T0194164

THE ALASTRINE LEGEND II

Also by Debbie Nordman:

The Alastrine Legend

THE ALASTRINE LEGEND II

Stormy Troubles

Debbie Nordman

THE ALASTRINE LEGEND II
STORMY TROUBLES

Copyright © 2014 Debbie Nordman.

All rights reserved. No part of this book may be used or reproduced by any means,
graphic, electronic, or mechanical, including photocopying, recording, taping or by any
information storage retrieval system without the written permission of the publisher
except in the case of brief quotations embodied in critical articles and reviews.

This is a work of fiction. All of the characters, names, incidents,
organizations, and dialogue in this novel are either the products
of the author's imagination or are used fictitiously.

iUniverse books may be ordered through booksellers or by contacting:

iUniverse LLC
1663 Liberty Drive
Bloomington, IN 47403
www.iuniverse.com
1-800-Authors (1-800-288-4677)

Because of the dynamic nature of the Internet, any web addresses or links contained in
this book may have changed since publication and may no longer be valid. The views
expressed in this work are solely those of the author and do not necessarily reflect the
views of the publisher, and the publisher hereby disclaims any responsibility for them.

Any people depicted in stock imagery provided by Thinkstock are models,
and such images are being used for illustrative purposes only.
Certain stock imagery © Thinkstock.

ISBN: 978-1-4917-4418-5 (sc)
ISBN: 978-1-4917-4420-8 (hc)
ISBN: 978-1-4917-4419-2 (e)

Library of Congress Control Number: 2014914768

Printed in the United States of America.

iUniverse rev. date: 09/16/2014

For my parents,
thank you for my life.

CONTENTS

# ACKNOWLEDGMENTS

I'D LIKE TO THANK MY family for their support, in particular, my husband who showed patience as I wrote.

I'd like to thank my friends who helped with editing my writing, making it better. I'd especially like to thank Sue Douglas. She encouraged me to publish my first book.

I'd like to dedicate my book to my parents, RW and Margaret Hanson. Thank you for your nurturing and parenting you gave me. You helped me grow into a person whose curiosity of the world is still very much alive.

CHAPTER 1

"Mom, can you tell Janna to shut up?"

"Tell Jared to stop yelling at me!"

"Okay," Angel said, "I've had enough, you two. You don't tell someone to 'shut up' and you know I don't like that. We are not arguing all the way to Falconland, are we?" She turned in her saddle and glared at the twins.

"No, Mom." Janna lowered her eyes. "I'm sorry."

"I'm sorry too," said Jared. He stole a quick glare at his sister. "I'll try to keep my temper in check."

She took notice of the twins' mounts. "Your arguing is making your ponies skittish. It'll serve you both right if you keep it up and end up on the ground. Your horses can give you punishment. I won't have to."

Riding alongside Angel, Avery glanced back and smiled. "You know she's right, children. So instead of arguing, both of you should be paying more attention to your surroundings. Use your senses more effectively. I'm going to ask you what you've seen and heard and smelled later, okay?"

"Yes, Dad," the twins said in unison. A smile crept onto their faces as they took their dad's advice.

Angel faced forward; her saddle creaked as she did so. She shook her head and harrumphed once. They were a blessing to her, but at times like these she'd rather have left them at home. Granted, they were usually very good. But they had the ability to test the patience of a tree, if that was even possible. *Maybe that's what they got from me*, she thought and chuckled. Avery and she had produced pretty children. The twins had inherited their father's blond hair, but had her red highlights. They had the typical pointed elfin ears. The rest of their features mirrored their mother's dainty and curious expressions. In fact, their curiosity was the one trait that got them into trouble all the time. Even so, thinking of them always made her proud.

Well, maybe they'll take their dad's suggestion to heart and try very hard to behave this time. And, she had to admit, the Lunn brothers and Ariel Ladora had helped to keep the children occupied on this trip.

She remembered the trouble they had gotten themselves into last year. While visiting Cornellius Fraomar, Cornellius's nephew, Nicholas had taken them hunting with him and she wasn't informed of the plan. The twins convinced Nicholas she had agreed to let them join him. While out in the swamp the three of them had gotten lost. If it wasn't for the twins' badgercat, Jamala, they would have met a certain death.

She sighed. Nice weather had followed them the entire trip. Today had been no exception. The afternoon proved cool and pleasant. She looked up at the sound of honking geese heading south and caught a glimpse of blue sky through a break in the forest canopy. Angel shook her head, enjoying the feel of her long auburn hair hanging loose for a change. She usually wore it in braids to keep the silky stuff in control, but not today. A breezy late autumn day was too tempting to tie it up. She told herself it could be her last day to enjoy it before winter set in.

She deeply inhaled the cool crisp air and let it out slowly. Winter was fast approaching. The horses' usual 'clip-clop' was a 'crunch-crunch' of dry leaves on the path. Soon the vibrant oranges and reds would become dull browns and grays.

Avery's silky voice cut into her musings. "Thinking of last time?" He reached over and took her hand into his.

She sighed. "Among other things, yes."

"Well, the children are older and wiser, eleven being a respectable age. Don't worry about them, Angel."

"I know." She sighed again. "I guess I should apologize too. I'm just worried about this speech Cornellius wants me to make for his coronation. I don't know what to say. What does a person do at one of these engagements?"

Avery laughed and released her hand. "Just be yourself. You know that's all Cornellius wants."

"Yeah." Angel rubbed her eyes. "Well, I guess I'd better think about what I'll say."

"I think we can all assist you on that." Avery slowed his horse down enough to draw even with the twins. "Children, your mom needs to concentrate on her speech. So, let's all help her out. Okay?"

"Okay," the twins said in unison. He stayed with them and kept them occupied with questions of what they had observed earlier. Plus, he talked about his boyhood times.

It sure is nice to hear the children enjoying themselves with their father, Angel thought, now leading the small band of elves. Though it had been fifteen years since her confrontation with Ahriman, she missed the companionship she had enjoyed with her twin, Alison, now known as Stormy. In Angel's mind, her sister "died" when the evil consciousness in Ahriman jumped into Alison and she became Stormy. Angel shook her head to clear it of the images of so long ago. Well, they would be at Damek tonight. The elves had taken their time traveling to the Falconland city, enjoying the autumn air. But the eighteen days of being on the road was wearing thin on Angel. She was looking forward to seeing Serylda and her family. The dwarves had been good friends over the years.

By the time they reached the city that evening, all were tired, including the four badgercats in the group. Their keen sense of solid ground had been a welcomed help in the swamps surrounding Falconland. All four were leading the company at the present time. Besides she couldn't leave Niedra at home. The big cat had saved Angel's life on numerous occasions. Her three kittens, nearly grown at a little over a year old, had been a blessing to the elves. The twins had adopted Niedra's firstborn kitten, Jamala, and Angel, knowing they would be safe as long as the three of them were together, had nothing to fear. The cat never left the twins' sight except to hunt. Otherwise, she made a pest of herself.

Merwyn and Derwyn Lunn, also twins, adopted the other two cats and named them Merr and Derr after themselves. Angel was glad of the brothers' company. It had taken her several months to tell them apart, although fifteen years had passed and she still got confused. Avery did it so easily, baffling her to this day. She knew he enjoyed her confusion in a loving way even though he never told her of it. That was just one of his many endearing traits she loved.

The gates of Damek appeared out of the swamps. The half-moon's light had been enough to help them locate the city's gates shortly after dusk. A sigh of relief echoed through the company when the doors opened and Cornellius stepped out.

"Welcome, my elfin friends," he said with a smile on his face and arms stretched wide. "I'm glad you made it. I was beginning to worry. My Coronation *is* tomorrow, you know."

The elves dismounted. The Lunn brothers took control of all the mounts as Angel and Avery strolled up to Cornellius, laughing and embracing their long-time friend. Ariel Ladora, Angel's aide, and the twins stayed near the horses, standing in front of the Lunn brothers. The other two elves in the company, Wyatt Keegan and Jarvis Baxter, stood behind the elfin king and queen. The four cats quietly sat on their haunches beside the horses who were used to their substantial size.

"We couldn't miss your coronation," Avery said, stepping back. "We just had a late start."

"Yes, and we brought Janna and Jared. Nicholas should be glad." Angel motioned them forward.

"Well, hello, you two." Cornellius shook both their hands. "I hope you both enjoy your stay without *troubling* anyone this time?"

The twins giggled. Jared glanced over at his sister and answered for them both. "We'll try, sir."

"Good." Cornellius grinned and turned back to Angel. The twins quickly and quietly went back to Ariel who nodded at Cornellius. Even with their tendency to get into trouble, the children never did like being in the center of attention.

Merwyn and Derwyn bowed slightly. Cornellius bowed back. Aware of the fact that the Lunn brothers shied away from physical contact, he didn't bother to shake their hands. Instead, he returned his attention back to Angel and Avery after nodding to Jarvis and Wyatt.

"I don't think Nicholas ever got over that fright he caused you two the last time you were here." Cornellius smirked and swept his left hand around. "As you can see, he didn't come to greet you. For a twenty-year old, he can be a little childish at times."

"Well, you can tell your nephew we don't carry grudges," Avery remarked.

Angel took a moment to release the cats' obligations and allowed them to go hunt in the swamps. Although she had the talent to speak to all four, she gave Niedra that task. Knowing her ability, the Lunn brothers never harbored jealousy toward Angel and allowed her to control their cats when the occasion called for it. As the animals trotted off into the darkness, she turned and took the hand Cornellius offered as he led them all inside the gates. The Lunn brothers gave up the six horses to the two Falconlanders waiting to take the animals to Damek's stables.

"You look good, friend," Angel said. "I think you've even filled out some, not quite as skinny as you used to be. And who did you allow to cut that mop of yours?" She reached up and tugged the ear-length locks that usually hung below his shoulders. The numerous street lamps muted the normally dirty-blond coloring.

He laugh quietly and ran his fingers through his hair. "Ah, you'll meet her soon enough, my lady." He took Angel's hand, placed it in the crook of his arm, and leaned close. "You see, I have a surprise for you. I'm getting married before the coronation."

"Well, that is a surprise," Avery exclaimed behind them. He chortled and slapped Cornellius on the back. "One I'm glad to hear. Believe me, if she's as good as Angel, you'll be blessed."

Angel laughed nervously. "Well, um, I can hardly wait to meet her. She must be something to be able to snatch one of the most stubborn bachelors around."

"Stubborn? Me?" Cornellius straightened and laughed heartily. "Angel, you sure make my day. Yes, my future wife is someone even you would approve of. Come on, everyone, I'll show you to your rooms for your stay here."

Angel enjoyed the stroll despite her tiredness. The streets were busy with people coming and going. The swamp on the other side of the city's wall was noisy with croaking frogs and chirping crickets. The swamp's mustiness and the salty breeze blended with the cooking odors coming from the houses they passed by.

"Have the dwarves arrived yet?" Avery asked.

"Oh, yes. They've been here for nearly a week now. Serylda is looking forward to seeing you, my lady. She says she misses you...I believe her exact word was 'immensely.' And speaking of her, here she is." Cornellius stepped away from Angel.

Serylda Blackstone, dressed as usual for a dwarf warrior in belted leather breeches, marched over and put her hands on Angel's upper arms. Minus her quarterstaff she was armed with a sheathed knife hanging from her belt. Angel smiled and gave her friend a bear hug.

"Angel, I'm sure glad to see you. How long has it been now? Four years?"

"Something like that." Angel pulled away and stole a glance at Cornellius. "Well, are you getting married like our friend here, or are you already married?"

Serylda grinned and shook her head. "Still trying to marry me off? Put yourself at ease, friend. I'm not going to mention who it is yet, but there is someone I'm serious about. Who knows, I may just get married too." The women went off to catch up on the latest happenings. As they left, Angel overheard Cornellius say something to the rest of the squad.

"There they go. That is true friendship. Well, I guess I'll take the rest of you to your lodgings. Serylda knows where that is, and she can show Angel."

The next morning Cornellius introduced his bride-to-be. Elena was tiny with raven-black hair and a strong personality, a good contrast to his fairness and easygoing nature. Angel saw at once how much Cornellius loved and cherished her when he took hold of her hand. They complemented each other nicely.

She gave Elena a grin and a sisterly hug, winking at Cornellius over Elena's shoulder. Sensing his need for her approval, Angel commented, "You'll let me know if Cornellius gets too wild, won't you."

Hearty laughter rang out. Cornellius laughed the loudest and knew all was well. He placed Elena's hand on his arm and led the others into the Great Hall.

Wreaths and both floor and wall sconces decorated the Great Hall for the festive occasion. The dwarf nation of Jasper had sent the specially molded sconces for the Coronation, made at Jasper's famous iron forges. The Bomani dwarves, not to be outdone, had fashioned elaborate metal wreaths decorated with evergreen vines, autumn leaves, and pine cones from the mountains surrounding Boman. The candles in the sconces had been the gift from Krikor, sent a few weeks earlier. The elves, while making them, had added floral essences from their realm to bring to the minds of everyone attending the festivities of this year's bountiful harvests.

They held the wedding in the Great Hall, a quiet affair with the elves and the Blackstone clan in attendance only. Ariel and the twins stayed in the children's room throughout the day's events. Though the twins were given the choice of participating in the Coronation, they opted out, not comfortable with crowds, which was unusual for their age. Quietly the musicians set up in the corner as to not disturb the ceremony. After the wedding, Cornellius and his new bride left to prepare for the Coronation. The doors to the Great Hall were opened, the musicians started playing while the people began entering the Hall.

While everyone waited for the happy couple to return, the people danced to the ballroom music. It turned out to be a colorful occasion. The women were clad in brightly rainbow-hued long-flowing dresses adorned with all sorts of beads and ribbons. Some even wore beads and ribbons in their hair to match. Others wore pointy hats with lots of "fluffy stuff" swirling down about them.

The men were dressed in simple brown or black breeches. The white shirts they wore reminded Angel of the pirate stories she was told of in her pre-teen years. The sleeves were overlarge to allow free movement of the men's shoulders and arms. Each of the males wore a belt that held a sword of some sort. Angel knew the weapons were polished to a shine though she couldn't see a single one. The men in this century never went without some kind of weaponry, even at fancy occasions as this.

The Coronation took place fifteen minutes later. The musicians began playing a marching tune signaling to the crowd that the ceremony was about to begin. The assembly grew quiet and parted, forming a central aisle. It spanned the entire length of the Great Hall, from the double doors at the south end to the north where the throne was situated atop a dais. The high priest of the land stood in front of the double-chaired throne. To the east and on the bottom step was Angel while Avery stood below her, at the same level as the crowd. The Lunn brothers and Nicholas stood with the assembly a few feet from Avery along with Wyatt and Jarvis.

Opposite them, Dwarflord Ganesh Blackstone stood on the same step as Angel, his consort Galinia mirrored Avery. Angel smiled and nodded at Ganesh and his wife who returned the gesture. Their heirs, Barak with his wife, Morna, Devlak, and their only daughter, Serylda, along with the rest of the dwarf company, stood in front with the assembly and to the west.

Angel's attention was brought back to the ceremony when the musicians slowed the tempo of their music and all conversation ceased. All eyes in the room turned toward the doors at the south. Two Falconlanders in highly decorated ceremonial dress stood at attention, their hands on the doorknobs. They opened the doors and twenty-four similarly dressed men marched in, the Home Guard. They took up equal positions down the length of the Great Hall. With a flourish, they unsheathed gleaming swords and held them high forming a silvery arch.

Cornellius, resplendent in gold and purple robes entered followed by his new consort, Elena, also dressed in gold and purple robes. They marched forward to the beat of the music and stopped at the bottom step leading to the throne. The entire assembly kept eyes upon the couple.

The music stopped.

Cornellius advanced up one step and stood below the high priest. A young lad of seven years came up on the west side and approached the priest. The lad carried a purple pillow on which a crown of gold and jewels rested. Behind him, a girl of the same age followed, also carrying a purple pillow and crown. Both children stopped beside the priest.

The priest took the crown from the boy's pillow and raised it over his head. Slowly, he lowered it onto Cornellius's head.

"I bless thee and thy kingdom, Cornellius Fraomar, High King of Falconland," the priest said loudly.

"Hail, King Fraomar!" the crowd cheered.

The newly appointed king stepped onto the dais while the priest moved over to stand to the east of the throne. The young boy marched over to stand beside the king's chair. The girl offered her crown to Cornellius who took it off the pillow. She turned and took up a similar spot opposite the boy next to the queen's chair.

Holding the crown high as the priest did, Cornellius waited as Elena took up the same space he stood when crowned. Slowly, he lowered the crown onto her head and said, "Behold, the High Queen of Falconland and my consort, Elena Fraomar."

"Hail, Queen Fraomar!" the crowd cheered.

Cornellius held out his hand and helped Elena up the remaining step. They walked to the throne, turned, and sat in unison. That signaled the Home Guard to lower and sheath their swords. The Home Guard, as one, stomped one foot and swiveled to face the throne. The high priest walked to stand in front of the new king and queen. He bowed low to them, turned, and walked off the dais. The children followed the priest. All three proceeded down the aisle between the Home Guard and disappeared out the double doors. The Home Guard made an about-face and followed. The two who stood guard at the doors were the last to leave, closing the doors as they did so.

Cornellius rose and introduced Angel to say a few words on his behalf. She made her way up and stood in front of the throne and bowed. The new king nodded and resumed his seat. Angel half-turned to face the crowd while she addressed Cornellius.

"Well, I won't lie, sir. I've been worried about what I could say that wouldn't make us both look like fools." She smiled and drew in a deep breath at the hesitant laughter that greeted her first words, then she gave the crowd her full attention. "This is my first Coronation. I know Falconland hasn't had a king and queen for over twenty years. Today is a new day for you. I believe in my heart Cornellius will rule wisely and justly. The Elfin Nation is proud to call him friend and ally. I also believe the Dwarf Nation agrees?" At Dwarflord Ganesh's nod, she continued.

"The Elfin Nation performs no such pomp and circumstance. As you all know, when I married Avery, we automatically became the elfin king and queen. Queen Kalika and King Iomar gave up the throne and left for unknown territory. We've tried to rule as they did." She turned back to Cornellius.

"I repeat, you are magnificent and Falconland is lucky to have such a man as you to rule over them. I give you our blessings, King Fraomar. May your new rule be full and with few problems." Facing the crowd once more, she raised her voice...

"Everyone, I give you the new king and queen of Falconland, Cornellius and Elena Fraomar!" Angel stepped down as the congregation cheered the new monarchy.

Suddenly the doors in the back of the Great Hall boomed open. At the same time Angel felt a familiar sensation she hadn't felt in fifteen years. A feeling of impending doom descended once more onto her shoulders as her heart beat faster. A Falconlander and a stranger marched up to the throne through the now-quiet assembly, still parted in the center.

"Sire, forgive me." The Falconlander bowed to his new king. "This is a messenger from Stormy. He has important news for everyone assembled here. I could not wait for the reception to bring him to you."

Cornellius rose and stepped forward. "What have you to say to us that couldn't wait, stranger?"

"First, my life means nothing. If you think I should die, so be it. Stormy gives you an ultimatum." The man paused and looked hard at

Cornellius who just stared at the man. Finally, as if coming to a decision, the stranger took a deep breath and continued. "She orders Angel to come to her at her south estate of Nemesis for discussions she didn't reveal to me. If she doesn't come, Stormy will destroy Krikor with a doomsday bomb. That ends my message. Don't ask me what she meant. I don't know myself."

The hall became noisy with the murmurs following the stranger's statement. Stunned, Angel collapsed down onto the steps leading up to the throne. Avery sat down beside her and placed one arm around her waist. Merwyn, standing nearby, laid a hand on her shoulder and a sense of sympathy flowed through his touch. She reached up and patted Merwyn's hand in acknowledgement before he stood back and released his hold.

She thought she had ended the business with Stormy and the "Alastrine Legend" nonsense. Fifteen years had convinced her that Stormy and Ahriman were something from her past and that they would stay in the past. That same amount of time also convinced her she no longer had a twin sister, that she was gone, too. Alison would forever remain Stormy. But now, Stormy was back and she had threatened her city with a doomsday bomb. *That has to be some sort of nuclear device,* she hypothesized to herself. *How did Stormy get a hold of something like that in this time?*

"Where is Stormy?" she asked aloud.

"Quiet, everyone!" Cornellius demanded. After the din died down, he asked, "What did you say, Angel?"

"Where's Stormy's so-called South Estate?"

The stranger bowed and said, "I've been granted the permission to give you that information. But I need a map to do so."

Cornellius dismissed the assemblage. Elena excused herself saying she would be visiting Angel's children. Dwarflady Galinia and Morna joined her. The newly appointed king led the way down the Great Hall to a door near the entrance that opened to a map room. Barak, along with the Lunn brothers and the Falconlander still escorting Stormy's man, followed Cornellius. Behind them came the rest of the elves and dwarves. Serylda joined Angel and Avery as they followed last. Avery excused himself and hurried to catch up to Barak.

Serylda stole a glance at Angel before she took hold of Angel's hand. "I'm sorry. But it looks like I'll get that chance to take my revenge on your sister. I'd hoped all that business had been finished. I guess I was wrong." She sighed. "I'm so sorry, Angel."

"Me, too, friend." Angel squeezed the dwarf's hand, feeling Serylda's empathy. "I had not forgotten the vow you had made years ago. I thought something had happened to Stormy in these past years. It saddens me to think we may have to kill my sister to get rid of the evil once and for all." She pulled away from the dwarf. "I need to think. Excuse me for a while. Please, tell everyone I'll be back and to not worry."

Angel fled past the map room and out the door. As she left, she saw Avery turn her way and Serylda place a hand on his arm arresting his move. She ran down the path that appeared on her left which she knew led to the People's Garden.

Is everything okay? she heard Avery ask in her mind.

I just need some time to think. I'm okay, Avery, she thought back to him.

Slowing her pace, Angel wandered the many cobblestone paths taking in the last scents of the season. The winding path she found herself on took her beside beds of herbs and plants gone dormant for the coming winter. A few late-bloomers like the colorful chrysanthemums left a splash of color among the gray stone benches along the path. One bench sat under a trellis full of grapevines heavy with ripe fruit.

She reached up and took a small bunch of grapes, sat down and popped one of the juicy, sweet morsels in her mouth. Savoring the fruity snack, Angel watched a busy bee visiting a white cushion mum nearby. She took a deep breath thinking the bees would be in hibernation by now and not out gathering nectar. Across from the path, the water grass and cattails stood in the center of a man-made pond surrounded by water lilies ready for winter. Angel wished she had been here when the lilies were in bloom. She remembered the lush reds, pinks, yellows, and whites of the summer flowers last year.

Angel groaned. The grapes had been refreshing but it didn't help her think. Tossing the stem from her snack into the brush, she rubbed her eyes before she stood and left the garden in search of her children.

Half an hour later, Avery found Angel in the children's room. Queen Elena, Dwarflady Galinia, and Morna were gone. The children were intently listening to their mother as she told them of the Coronation. Ariel sat next to her and looked up. He placed a finger to his lips. Her eyebrows raised, Ariel smiled and returned her attention back to Angel.

Jamala sat at the twins' feet. Niedra was nowhere to be seen. *She's out hunting with Merr and Derr,* Angel thought to him.

When she finished her tale, she turned her attention to Avery. The twins beamed up at him but stayed where they were seated.

"We're needed back at the Great Hall."

"Not the map room?" Angel rose.

"Apparently, the messenger was hungry. When you disappeared, Cornellius had the map spread out on the Great Hall floor. He thought it wise not to let the stranger see any more than he already had." They left the room hand in hand while Ariel remained with the children.

Back at the Great Hall, Angel's friends of so long ago surrounded the map on the floor. She chuckled to herself despite the dread she felt as she joined them at the map. It was just like that day in Krikor when Ahriman threatened them. At least this time she was a part of the group, not the legendary figure they believed would defeat the evil in their world. After the stranger pointed out the whereabouts of Stormy's location, the Falconlander led him away.

"Okay, what have we got?" she asked. Niedra padded up to her, purring loudly, back from hunting. Angel absentmindedly petted the big cat's head. The Lunn brothers' cats were still out.

"Well, Stormy's new haunt is south and west of here, about twenty-five to thirty days' march." Barak pointed to the spot.

Angel examined it and her mind came up with the uncanny feeling of knowing the area, of being there as a child. She studied the map closer. The area reminded her of a trip she had taken with her parents so long ago. She sighed. Had time erased all signs of the Alamo of San Antonio? Did Stormy take possession of one of the many cavern systems around there?

Serylda touched Angel's arm. "What's wrong?"

"Just thinking of my childhood and missing my parents." Angel drew in a deep breath and let it out. "I'm okay. Does anyone know of an ancient city around there?"

"Yes," Cornellius answered. "Wild animals, including bears, had pretty much taken control of that entire area the last time I was there, including some caverns. If you need to find them, I may be able to locate them. I can't guarantee it, though."

"How long ago was it when you were there?" Avery asked.

Cornellius smiled wryly. "Quite a while ago. I'd say twenty years or more." He frowned. "Angel, you know the area, don't you?"

Angel nodded. "My parents had taken us on a vacation to see the Alamo. It was a mission, a combination church and fort, in a city called San Antonio. Are there any signs of the city?"

"Some foundations still appear out of the brush near a river. There was a city in the area but the buildings were cannibalized for construction elsewhere." Cornellius thought a moment while he studied the map. "But that's all I remember."

"What is this 'Alamo' you speak of?" Dwarflord Ganesh asked.

"A little over 100 years before my time a famous massacre had ensued where only a very few people survived," Angel said. "'Remember the Alamo' was a famous saying because the people inside the fort fought an army of thousands, unwilling to give up."

Cornellius straightened up from leaning over the map. "I haven't thought of that area in a long time, since I traveled there in my youth. It was my first trip as a newly appointed scout, a test if you like." He snorted and added, "Although my father had accompanied me."

Angel sighed as she looked at the faces surrounding her. Everyone in attendance knew of her past life. Angel had informed them of it after the Ahriman business fifteen years ago. There were the dwarves, Ganesh and his children, Barak, Devlak, and Serylda. The elves next to her were Avery and the Lunn brothers. And, Cornellius, the newly appointed monarch of Falconland, stood across from her. The spouses of Ganesh, Barak, and Cornellius were absent. On the way back to the Great Hall earlier, Avery and Angel had met up with the three women. They left to visit the twins and Ariel, having enjoyed their youthfulness before the Coronation that morning.

After a moment Angel said, "I remember some of the cavern systems near the ancient city. In my old time, we called the one north of the city Natural Bridge Caverns of Texas. It isn't very big. But it would give Stormy plenty of space. It had lots of water and vegetation. And a major road passed by there, if I'm not mistaken. I was pretty young, before the tornado that took my parents. Is it like that now, Cornellius?"

"What I remember of it, yes. It's a perfect place if she had slaves to aid her. That is, if the caverns are still there as you remember them."

"I'm sure she had plenty slaves to do her bidding," Serylda retorted. "I'll bet that's the place she's made as Nemesis."

Suddenly Angel felt uneasy. *What is bothering me, now? It's not Serylda's attitude. It's coming from me.* No, it was her crystal hanging around her neck. It was warm to her skin. This same crystal had gotten her into so much trouble before she understood it. What was it telling her now? Was it glowing? She kept it hidden from view. She didn't like to advertise its uniqueness.

When Queen Kalika first gave her the crystal, it just glowed for her so she kept it hidden. Of course, Queen Kalika had told her to do so. Later, she began developing the ability to read thoughts not her own, even those from wild badgercats. She still had that ability and had learned to harness it when she needed it. Her children didn't inherit the ability, a blessing to Angel. Everyone in the room knew of the crystal and her unique gift. They all trusted her and knew she'd never invade their privacy unless absolutely necessary.

"People," she began, "I've got an uneasy feeling coursing through my body. I think my crystal is trying to tell me something. There's more than the doomsday bomb. I don't know what. But it's something very bad."

An elf from Krikor entered the Great Hall. Limping from hastily bandaged wounds, he reached Avery and went down onto one knee, swaying with the effort. "Sire, Krikor is under siege." And with those words, the elf fell over, took one last breath, and died.

After commanding two of his men to gently take the dead elf away, Cornellius decided to have a talk with the man in the city's prison. Barak elected to join him.

The feeling of panic Angel experienced nearly overwhelmed her. She feared the future and what it held for her this time.

CHAPTER 2

Stormy Troubles

CORNELLIUS AND BARAK RETURNED FROM questioning Stormy's man in Damek's prison. Barak looked ready to do battle and moved away from everyone, ignoring the faces studying him. Cornellius just shook his head and addressed the gathering.

"My guards will keep him under watch, so that's one who won't bother us again. By the way, Angel, he said Stormy intends to destroy all elves whether you see her or not. He said she was going to use that bomb on Krikor after killing as many as she could with her army. He was instructed to keep that tidbit secret for a while."

Angel gasped. "Why would she do that?" She closed her eyes and groaned. "I need to talk to the Ancient Ones, if any yet live. They may be able to help us since Stormy is possessed by their ancient enemy."

"I'm going with you," Serylda interjected.

"We should all go," Avery said, and then added, "But I think we should leave the children here."

"My nephew can take care of them." Cornellius grinned. "It's a good way for him to show you how responsible he's become. I don't think he'd let them get away with anything this time."

"I agree." Avery nodded his head and looked over at Angel. "And let us not forget, Jamala is here."

"Ariel can stay here and keep them occupied. It may keep them out of trouble." A thought occurred to Angel. She turned around. "Devlak, I have a favor to ask of you, if it's okay with Dwarflord Ganesh."

When she glanced his way, the dwarflord nodded.

She turned her eyes back to Devlak, "Please take Merwyn and Derwyn to Boman and beg help from Dwarflord Boden Greyrock for my people."

Devlak bowed. "I am honored to do your bidding, my lady. We will get your people to safety." The Lunn brothers nodded their agreement. With the danger ahead, all knew the Lunn brothers' two badgercats would be insurance on their journey. The three men headed out immediately.

"We should leave now too," Barak said.

"I'll round up the supplies we need," Cornellius added.

Angel and Avery, assured that everything was being taken care of for the journey, left to be with their children as long as possible before they had to go. Dwarflady Galinia, Queen Elena, and Morna were sent to their respective husbands. Ariel was asked to stay. They told the three what was about to transpire. Angel knew what the reaction of her children would be at the information. The twins weren't happy to be staying behind.

"Don't leave us here. We could stay at Jasper," Janna whined.

Jared agreed with his twin. "Yeah, and you had promised you'd take us to see the Great Crack."

"Not this time, children," Angel said. "We need you to stay and behave. It will be too dangerous to take you along with us."

"That does not mean stay until you two decide not to," Avery added.

Both children lowered their heads. Their parents smiled at each other, knowing what was on the twins' minds.

Ariel assured them the children would be fine. "Besides, what kind of trouble can they get into with Jamala, Nicholas, and myself watching over them? Good luck, my lady. Sir." After exchanging hugs and reassurances, Angel and Avery left the twins in Ariel's competent hands.

Two hours later the company left Damek on horses. Knowing time was essential, even the dwarves rode, not their favorite mode of transportation. Riding with Angel and Avery were the two elfin scouts, Jarvis Baxter and Wyatt Keegan. Dwarflord Ganesh and his wife, Galinia led their family, Serylda, Barak, and Barak's wife, Morna. Since the company would be passing near Jasper, both Galinia and Morna chose to accompany their husbands. The women were ready to go home. Cornellius Fraomar and two of his men, Alec Huntley and Colin Barrett with their falcons, represented the Falconlanders. Cornellius chose them because he had lost his faithful bird a year ago and hadn't had the time to train a new one. Though very young and still in training, the men's two birds were noted for their hunting abilities. Niedra the badgercat sniffed out danger along the way.

They agreed the fastest way to Jasper and the Great Crack beyond entailed traveling due west. The benefit was being drier than and not quite as cold as following the Red River farther north from their present location. The only drawback? They would be traveling uncomfortably close to Stormy's new locale, about two days from their intended route. Everybody took care of their own water, while the horses carried extra provisions and water.

Traveling hard the company enjoyed good weather. Sunshine and warm temperatures followed them. Six days into the journey found the company traversing a swampy region, an area not too familiar to Angel.

"Where is this swamp on your map, Barak?" Angel asked. Thinking back to her childhood she had a feeling it was the ancient state line between Texas and Louisiana. She couldn't remember the river's name, though she faintly remembered a wetland her family had visited long ago.

After retrieving his map, Barak spread it on a dry spot on the ground. "We're approximately here, in the Crimson Marsh."

"Thanks." Yes, they were where Angel thought. "How far do we have to go yet?"

Barak pondered a moment before answering her. "In about ten more days we'll be north of Stormy's caverns."

"We need to be sure we don't end up there before we're ready," Avery said.

"If we keep to our route, we should miss her haunt by about a day's ride."

"Thanks, Barak. I hope you're right." Angel straightened up and looked around. "We should probably refill our water skins if we can find good water."

"I remember a place nearby with good-tasting water coming from a rock," Cornellius added as Barak returned the map to its pouch on his horse.

The company remounted and Cornellius led them a mile south to the spring he remembered as having good water. After everyone drank their fill and topped off their skins the trek resumed.

Five days later they passed by the ruins of an ancient city. Angel knew it as Austin. They traveled with no mishaps. As Barak had predicted, they were only a day from Nemesis, if the Natural Bridge Caverns were indeed Stormy's Nemesis. Niedra roamed outside the camps with one of the four scouts taking turns guarding the camp center during their nightly stops.

They halted around noon and held a meeting after coming across a recent campfire beside an ancient road.

"Where are we?" Angel asked. "Barak, we need to see your map again."

Barak took one out of his pack and spread it out on the ground. Everyone dismounted and gathered around the map. Niedra went off in her habit to check out the immediate area.

"We are here." Cornellius pointed to a place on the map. "I am a little more familiar with this area. I remember my father speaking of some trouble here a few decades ago. The caverns are indeed south of here."

"Then we need to be extra vigilant," Avery interrupted. "We're dangerously close to Stormy's new haunt."

Angel sighed. "I agree. How close are we to Jasper, Cornellius?"

"Perhaps another five days' ride. I guess we should think of making camp soon."

"Not here," said Wyatt suddenly.

Angel frowned at the elf. Wyatt rarely said anything, his trademark. "Why not?"

"I feel danger nearby. And Niedra is still missing."

Avery scanned the area. "You're right. I wonder where she is."

Angel used her mental ability to scan for Niedra. She found her a few yards to the left. The cat sent her back a feeling of danger and caution.

In the meantime she heard Barak comment. "I sure wish that dratted cat wouldn't do that. It still makes me nervous even though it's saved my life once. Shouldn't it be back by now?"

Angel turned to Barak. "She's nearby and senses danger, too. Everyone please be on your guard. I think we need to ready our weapons."

As everyone digested her words, Dwarflord Ganesh spoke up. "I don't know about the rest of you but I prefer that cat to be in sight."

At that moment he looked over at Angel, astonishment mirrored in his face. He glanced down at the arrow sticking through his chest before collapsing to the ground, his hand on his ax still sheathed. His wife Galinia screamed and rushed to his side in vain. The arrow had pierced his heart. He died in her arms, missing the chance to die a dwarf warrior with weapon in hand.

The company transformed into a fighting unit. The elves nocked arrows and the dwarves and Falconlanders removed sheathed swords amid the swishing arrows coming from the rocky terrain. Miraculously avoiding the rain of arrows, Serylda moved Galinia and Morna into cover before joining the fray. Her quarterstaff still with her horse, she fought with her sword, always strapped to her side. Angel, armed only with her quarterstaff, joined the two women to protect them. Thankful that she had used it for a walking stick, she fought any enemy who came too close to her and the two she safeguarded. Too confused and inexperienced in battle to help, the two young falcons retreated to hide in the trees.

Soon the dwarves had routed the ambushers out of hiding and the fighting turned to hand-to-hand combat. Since Angel only carried the staff, she stayed where she and the two older women hid. Watching from the cover of the brush, she heard another sound pierce the air. Niedra smashed into the fray and tore several men apart before Angel rushed out and took control of the cat. She needed survivors for questioning. At this rate no enemy fighter would be alive. In the end, one man barely hung on by the time Niedra calmed down. The man, barely alive due to the gashes he endured from the cat, lay on the ground near the fire pit.

"Who sent you?" Barak barked. When the man didn't answer, Barak shook him. "Where did you come from?"

"Easy, Barak," Angel said. She calmly and lightly tapped his shoulder once. "He can't talk if he's dead."

Barak shook the man once more and let him slump to the ground. He moved off to join his family. Angel felt the disgust in Barak and hoped he hadn't killed their only source of information.

She squatted next to the injured man. Using her staff for balance she quietly asked him, "Who is your commander?" When the man didn't answer she added, "You may as well tell us. We both know you're bleeding to death. Will telling me now matter?"

"Stormy," he whispered. With an evil laugh, he drew his last breath and died.

Angel stood and faced west. "I desperately need to get to the Great Crack as quickly as possible."

"Angel." Serylda's soft voice captured Angel's attention. She was kneeling beside a wounded Avery and tears quietly flowed down her cheeks. "We need to get our wounded to Jasper first."

Angel rushed to her husband's side to check his wounds. Serylda rose and moved off to her family. Why hadn't she sensed his agony? His eyes were clamped shut from the obvious pain. Using her gift she softly probed him.

Avery? How bad is it?

Don't worry about me, my love. I will survive though I'm in extreme pain at present. It's more important for you to find out the reason behind Stormy's reappearance.

Yes, but…

No, he argued. *You again have a job to perform which we are merely here to help you. I am not so wounded you need to worry.*

Very well, my dear elf. I sense that your wounds are not life-threatening and will let you be.

Angel smiled down at her husband, warmed by his strength. She thanked the Maker he wasn't seriously hurt and knew he wasn't going to be able to fight for a few weeks. Turning her thoughts elsewhere, she looked over at Serylda who had joined her mother and sister-in-law. All three were sitting beside the late dwarflord.

"How many died, Serylda?" Angel asked, knowing the dwarf held that information. Her voice was hushed in deference of their loss.

"We lost Jarvis, Collin, Alec, and my father. Mother is wounded. And so are Avery and Wyatt." Serylda turned and allowed Angel to see her tears, a thing no dwarf usually did. "The wounded need attention soon or they may die as well from infections."

"Someone needs to rush back to Damek," Wyatt succeeded in moaning.

"No! To Jasper," cried Galinia. She slumped down next to her dead husband. "To Jasper," she whispered, grief-stricken. Morna sat next to her in shock. Serylda stood and backed away, no longer crying.

Taking his sister's place, Barak laid a gentle hand on both his mother and wife. "I agree. We need to go to Jasper. Damek lies in the wrong direction." He looked intently at Angel willing her to see his thoughts, to understand him. She nodded and embraced his thoughts as he rose and went to work.

She had to think, get away from the battle. Angel moved away from everyone but stayed in sight. No one bothered her. She sensed their understanding of her need to be alone.

Why was Stormy doing this? Why did she return now? Angel had accepted the hard truth that she had lost her sister fifteen years ago. Why couldn't she stay hidden? Did this mean she hadn't finished her work as the Alastrine Savior? The Legend had said she'd defeat the evil of Ahriman. Did she not do that? He was gone. But, was the "evil" really gone? Her sister Alison, turned into the heartless Stormy when Ahriman had taken control of her. That had been a hard time for Angel. It took these past fifteen years for Angel to accept this loss of her sister. Now, she found herself thrown back into a similar turmoil.

Angel mulled over the battle scene. The two young falcons, now alone, stood over their masters, dead from numerous arrows. All the ambushers lay dead from Niedra's mauling or her comrades' weapons. As she watched, Cornellius and Barak gathered the dead for burial, one pile for their own and another for the enemy. They dug two ditches and piled the dead in them. They covered their comrades' bodies with the dirt. The other pit was put to flame. The women concentrated on patching the injured. Finished with the grisly task he and Barak performed, Cornellius took control of the two falcons, putting them on his horse. Angel felt his temporary acceptance of the birds as his own.

Returning to her thoughts, Angel had to ask herself if there was anything left of Alison in Stormy. Did the evil entity Angel had chased from Ahriman still live inside Alison? Was that the reason she was being forced to confront the same evil? For that is what she truly felt, that it was the same evil. She desperately needed to talk to Kalika. She needed to know what kind of malevolence they were confronting. Angel sighed and returned to the company, her mind in worse confusion than before.

"We have hard choices to make, my friends," she said. Everyone turned their attention to the Alastrine Savior. "Serylda, with Barak's okay, I want you to rush ahead to Jasper and bring back help. When you return, I will head to the Great Crack as quickly as I can."

Barak nodded. "I agree. Serylda, we'll ready the wounded and follow you. Hurry back with help, my sister."

Serylda jumped onto their swiftest horse and was off. Angel made sure she had plenty of provisions for both herself and the horse before allowing Serylda to leave. Watching as Serylda rode away Angel felt relieved the dwarves were accustomed to riding though they didn't enjoy the prospect.

The wounded were each placed upon stretchers made from ropes hastily woven between a set of poles and cushioned with leaves and grasses. Each stretcher was strapped behind a horse led by one of the four remaining members of the overwhelmed company. With the dead buried and Barak in the lead, the company headed off immediately. Although twilight was upon them, everyone wanted to begin the arduous journey ahead. The full moon gave them enough light to see throughout the night.

Lower temperatures and a light snow met them the next day and slowed them down a little. The injured made Angel promise not to stop on their account. The more they traveled, the quicker medical attention would arrive. Angel slowed their pace a little instead of camping for the day.

Angel sent a prayer of thanks for the good weather they sustained after that one day of snow. Even so, she feared they wouldn't make Jasper in time to save Galinia and Wyatt. Both began suffering infections in their wounds. With Barak's help, Angel found herbs to slow the infections. And the company trudged on.

On December 4, three days by horse from Jasper, Serylda showed up with a contingency of dwarves and wagons. Somehow, Galinia and Wyatt held on, though barely. She forgot how stout the people were in this day and age. Her fear of losing them turned out to be unwarranted. After the doctors tended the wounded, they headed out. Angel and Serylda left the company in good hands.

Serylda insisted on accompanying Angel and brooked no argument. Furthermore, Angel had tried to make Niedra stay with the company to no avail. Avery sided with the cat and convinced her to take it.

"We have the dwarf army to get us to Jasper. You two need her more than we, my love." He held Angel's hand a moment before they were off.

Angel's tears fell freely. Serylda said nothing, deeply mourning the loss of her father though she didn't show it by crying this time, her dwarven senses again in control. They headed for the Great Crack with about 900 miles of traveling to go. On horseback, they would reach their destination in a little over two weeks according to Serylda.

Three days later they passed Jasper. They told the lookout the wagons with the wounded traveled about five walking days behind them. They didn't stop having more than 600 miles yet to go.

"I wish these were better times," Serylda remarked. "You haven't been here in several years."

"I know. I have no excuse either, my dear friend." Angel sighed. "Tell me, why are you going with me this time?"

"I had told you long ago I would help the Alastrine Savior no matter the circumstances. And, since you still are this person, you cannot leave me behind."

"Yes you did. And you haven't disappointed me yet. You are truly named, Battle-maid." She sighed once more. "I wonder what the Ancient Ones will tell me. That is, if any still live."

"They die, too?" Serylda asked, surprised. "I thought they were immortal. That's what our legends say."

Angel chuckled. "I wish it were so, my friend. But everything dies, even the Ancient Ones." She urged her mount into a gallop. Serylda followed suit.

⎯⎯⎯ᴠᴠ∘ᴏᴇ⭙ᴏᴏ⭙ᴇ∘ᴏᴠᴠ⎯⎯⎯

Both were tired and dirty. December was nearly over and their destination lay a day away. At least the weather had been good. They suffered neither rain nor snow on their long ride. Their days were filled with riding, only to stop when needs arose. Their nights consisted of their one meal for the day and Niedra watching over them as they slept. The cat had the ability to sleep, awakening when danger loomed nearby. Only once did they find themselves in danger of being found by a couple of feral badgercats. With Niedra's forewarning, Angel managed to send the cats on a false trail.

Serylda found a secluded spot surrounded by shrubs and boulders for their last campsite before reaching the Great Crack. The day proved to be pleasant despite the wind they endured for December 21. But when the sun sank below the horizon, the cold of early winter replaced the warmth of the day.

At least the wind had died, Angel thought with thanksgiving.

As she readied a fire for their meal, Serylda left to hunt. Niedra, back from her own hunt, relaxed a little away from the fire pit and concentrated on her meal. The fire blazed bright and warm when Serylda returned with a small rabbit in her hand, dressed and ready to cook. She had cleaned the meat outside of camp to keep any scavengers away, as she had done their entire trip.

After their repast, they sat quietly near the fire and relaxed with steaming mugs of coffee. Niedra strolled up and laid down behind Angel. When the cat began to purr, Angel knew they were safe for the moment. She took a sip of the coffee and leaned back against the big cat, closing her eyes and enjoying the animal's warmth. "I hope Queen Kalika is still alive, especially if none of the others are."

Serylda jerked herself upright from the boulder she leaned against. "What did you just say? Queen Kalika?" She frowned but smiling with sudden insight she added, "She's one of the Ancient Ones. Deny it."

Angel looked over at her friend. "I guess it's time to tell you a little elfin history." She pointed and frowned at Serylda. "But I want your promise on your honor as a dwarf that you won't repeat anything I'm about to tell you. That is, unless Kalika or myself allow you to break this promise."

"You have my word." Serylda gave the dwarf sign of honor before she took a sip of her coffee and leaned back, ready to hear the tale.

Angel closed her eyes and began. "A long time ago, as you know, people from another world arrived on our planet. They saw the damage we were inflicting on the earth and knew we were destroying our only home and turning it into one unable to support life. The Centauri were a peaceful people and wanted to help us. So they set out to do just that. Shortly thereafter, one of their own disappeared. They never found him."

"Ahriman, right?" Serylda, like all dwarves, enjoyed listening to history, whether or not they'd heard the particulars before.

Angel nodded. "He reappeared telling the world he would destroy everything if he wasn't worshiped as a god. Nobody listened. So, he set off a nuclear device on their ship, destroying it and all hopes of leaving this world. Seeing this in the heavens, it was believed a bomb in space had been detonated. The nations of the world went to war, not realizing it had been Ahriman who caused the bright star-like vision to form. Each nation in turn blamed the others for the devastation that followed. As of today, we still don't know how the other side of the world fared."

Angel sat upright and crossed her legs. Both girls took a swallow of their coffee before Angel continued.

"Earlier you guessed right. Queen Kalika was the youngest of the Ancient Ones, or Centauri, their real names. It was thrust upon her to begin the Legend and save some of the humans still living at the time. She chose the name Alastrine because it meant 'savior of man.' She fled to what you know now as Krikor with a handful of humans, both male and female and bred with the men, producing the first elves. The elves decided that in order to truly live free, the beginning of their race needed to be forgotten. In time, only her consorts ever knew of her identity. She's been on this world for 2000 years more or less."

"Queen Kalika didn't look that old."

Angel chuckled. "I asked her how they kept the secret. She told me but I promised her I wouldn't divulge that information. I will let her decide if you should know. For now, be content to know her true identity. And, since you do know, your dwarf honor comes into play."

"Yes, ma'am. I understand." Serylda held her right hand to her breast. "I will take this information to my grave. As you said earlier, only Queen Kalika or you can release me from this vow." She rose with those words and refilled their mugs with the remaining coffee and sat back down.

Angel stared at the fire after taking a sip of her coffee. She gathered her thoughts together, leaned back against Niedra, her purring comforting to Angel.

"I've changed my mind. I know how much you take pride in your honor. I will tell you more," she said. She looked over at Serylda who again made the dwarf sign of honor.

"The Centauri had a power that enabled them to travel through time. But that carried a heavy price. It took from their long life span. For every year they travel in time, they lose two years of regular life. Four Centauri offered to go back in time. They brought Alison and myself forward twenty years to the time they had initially arrived on this planet. They discussed how they would explain our appearance in the future. It was then that Kalika was given charge to begin the Legend you are so familiar with. She only knew the approximate time when we'd turn up by guessing how much time was available from the Centauri who brought us forward. She was given the crystal I now wear to keep it safe until I arrived. The crystal came from their home world. A drop of my blood was placed upon the crystal before it was encased in something to keep it protected through time. In this fashion the peoples of today would know I am the true Savior. The effects it had on me weren't anticipated."

"Your change in appearance and the mind reading?" Serylda drank what was left in her mug and put it in front of her.

Angel nodded and finished her coffee. She placed her mug on the ground next to Serylda's mug. "After they took my blood, two others brought us as far forward in time as their life span would allow. They gave up their lives hoping to give the remaining Centauri a chance to correct what they felt was their mistake."

Angel stopped her narration long enough for the girls to ready themselves for the night. Serylda took the mugs and put them inside her pack while Angel retrieved four blankets from the horses. The dwarf took one and laid it out on the ground near the fire. Angel placed the other three on a corner of the same blanket. Both girls sat down upon the opened one as Serylda had a question wanting answered.

"What did you mean by the Centauri having a mistake? What was that?"

"They felt it had been their fault one of their own people killed. Any killing was abhorrent to them. For Ahriman to do what he did shook them up badly. They felt they should try to rectify this error before relying on me. As you know, they weren't successful, hence I'm in the 'picture' as the saying goes. You know the rest."

Serylda nodded. "Yeah, my brothers found you and your sister wandering our halls. But, if they left you in Jasper, where did they go?"

Angel thought a moment, her eyebrows rose. "Good question. I never thought about that. Perhaps they found a deep chasm and threw themselves in so as to not be discovered. I think I'll ask Kalika if she knows anything about that."

Serylda shrugged. "That would explain why no one has found any bodies to this day."

Angel took a deep breath and let it out slowly. "As you know, I defeated Ahriman. Only I didn't destroy the evil inside him. It lingered on and is now lurking inside my sister."

"And this is why you need to talk to Queen Kalika about destroying this 'evil' and saving your sister."

Angel nodded. "You know me all too well, my dwarf friend. I can't give up hope that she can still be saved. Especially now that she's back in my thoughts."

Serylda rose and gathered the three blankets. "I often wondered where Queen Kalika and King Iomar went when you and Avery took up the elfin crowns. My dwarf heart so desires to see this cavern system where the Ancient Ones reside."

Angel helped Serylda spread the three blankets over the one they had sat upon. The girls crawled under them, settling down for the night. The girls huddled together for warmth in the chilly night air, backs next to each other. Niedra padded over and laid nearby, keeping watch as only wild animals can, able to do so even in sleep.

"I hope you can, too. The last time we were here, Avery wasn't allowed inside even though he is elf. He didn't know the story back then. But since you now know the story, Queen Kalika may allow it." Angel laugh quietly. "Well, that is if anyone is still alive. Time seems to stand still inside the cave."

The dwarf nodded. "I remember how surprised you were when you learned how long you'd been gone."

Still smiling, Angel replied, "It *was* a little unnerving." She stared into the fire, slowly turning to embers.

"I have one more question. How many years do the Centauri live?"

"I was told by Kalika they can be anywhere from 4000 to 5000 earth years old."

"No wonder we think they're immortal. That is a long time."

"Yes," Angel agreed as she settled into the blankets. "I guess we'd better get some sleep. Tomorrow is a big day."

No sooner had Serylda bid her goodnight, Angel heard snoring coming from her friend. She wasn't quite ready to fall asleep. Her thoughts turned to the Great Crack. Eager to finish this leg of their journey, she hoped the queen and king were still alive. So many questions tumbled through her mind as she finally drifted off.

———⁓⁓⟋⊙⊙⟋⊙⊙⟍⁓⁓———

"We're back," Angel said as they looked over the great expanse that once was called the Grand Canyon.

The women looked out upon a vastness that still had the ability to take their breaths away. Two thousand years did little to the majestic gorge the Colorado River had cut in the earth.

One thing more remained to do before setting up camp. It had taken the women until noon to reach the chasm. They needed to find their old campsite. Serylda assured Angel she could find it, a trick dwarves were famous for and one Angel was thankful for. Hopefully it wouldn't take long. Angel began to realize how much she missed her husband and children, hoping Avery's injuries were healing and her children were still safe in Damek. The problem facing the women now? How far east or west did they need to go to find the old campsite?

CHAPTER 3

The Great Crack

A NGEL SQUINTED OVER THE EXPANSE and noted the slight rise that cut off the view of the canyon. To her, everything looked the same. The sprinkling of snow hadn't yet melted and gave a nice luster to the area. *I wonder why there isn't more snow for this time of year*, she thought.

"I hope this doesn't take much longer." Angel said aloud and sighed. "I just wish I could remember where we camped the last time we were here. Are you sure we're going the right way?"

"I know where we need to be," Serylda said confidently and led Angel further west.

"How? It was fifteen years ago." Angel looked around as she followed her friend. "It all looks the same to me."

Serylda stared over the horizon. "It was the last time I saw Javas alive."

How could Angel forget that? Stormy, being possessed by Ahriman, had made a surprise attack upon the camp while she was talking to the Ancient Ones. When she returned to camp, the only ones she found were Barak and Serylda, both hurt and Barak barely alive. The remainder of their group had been captured or killed. The girls left Barak and went after Stormy who was on her way to Attor. On the mad dash to catch up to Stormy, the girls came across several campsites. One of them held a terrible surprise. Javas Ozuna, an elf betrothed to Serylda, had been brutally killed. The blood revenge Serylda vowed that day held the same strength today. When a dwarf made such a vow, only death satisfied it, a trait all dwarves shared no matter the gender. Angel didn't have to probe her friend's mind to know it hadn't abated with time.

"I'm sorry I'd forgotten." She beckoned Serylda on when the dwarf looked back at her.

Angel's horse followed the sure-footed steps of Serylda's mount. It wasn't long before the dwarf stopped and dismounted. Angel followed suit and looked around. She felt Serylda's eyes follow her and smiled back at her friend.

"I remember this spot. Do you remember how frightened I was with the knowledge that I had to go down into that void?" Angel gestured toward the canyon.

Serylda grinned. "I sure do. I'm glad you aren't like that now. Avery isn't here. He was able to help you overcome that problem. I'm afraid I don't have that ability. I only know how to take care of my own faults."

Angel nodded. "It had helped when fog enshrouded the canyon and I couldn't see the bottom." She looked skyward a moment. "Well, it's not quite noon. Let's hunt out the cave now. We can leave Niedra with the horses. She'll take care of them."

After Angel held a silent conversation with her cat, the girls began the descent into the canyon. Confidently and sure-footed, Angel led them down. She thought it strange she remembered the way as if it happened yesterday and not years ago. *And yet, I couldn't remember the area we had camped that fateful day,* she thought as she pointed out a squirrel scampering in the sunshine ahead of them. Below, they both spotted the sheep jumping from ledge to ledge.

Half an hour later they stood in front of a pile of brush and rocks. The light snow surrounding them had melted around the brush and left the ground soggy. Angel glanced up when she realized she felt the sun's warmth on her back.

"Before we start clearing this brush away, I'd like to make sure Queen Kalika is still alive." Serylda nodded in acknowledgement as Angel closed her eyes.

My queen, can you hear me? Angel thought to her.

Loud and clear, my child. Kalika's thoughts held amusement. *We've been waiting for your arrival.*

Angel chortled to herself. *How long have you known we were coming? Think. You know the answer.*

She considered a moment and identified the time Kalika meant. *At Damek, My crystal.*

Very good, Angel.

I have Serylda with me. She knows your secret. May she enter also? It is allowed.

Angel opened her eyes and looked at Serylda. "Well, my friend, we have permission. Let's get busy. We've been invited inside."

The girls spent the next hour clearing the debris away from the entrance that thirteen years had deposited. As they worked, Angel thought on the years she and Avery had ruled since escorting the old queen and king here. They had enjoyed peace and brought their twins into the world. She wished this visit would have been a pleasant one and not one where she needed the queen's help.

Angel noted the smile on Serylda's face when they uncovered the cave opening. "Don't tell me you're surprised. Didn't you trust me?"

"Well, yes." Serylda glanced down then back up at Angel. She shook her head. "To be honest, not really."

Angel couldn't help herself. The opportunity to tease her friend came up so seldom she didn't want to pass it up. "You know, maybe I'm wrong about this being the entrance. The queen's thoughts did seem farther away." She looked around. "Perhaps we've cleared the wrong spot. What do you think?"

"What?" Serylda frowned. "There is no way I'd know where to look. You know that."

Angel pursed her lips to keep from laughing. "I had hoped, you being a dwarf, you'd see some clue in the soil to confirm my decision."

"I may be a dwarf, but you know I still need to be at a place to find it again."

Angel snickered and Serylda glared at her. "You were surprised I knew this was the entrance. Don't deny it."

Serylda's glare turned into a grin. "Ha, ha to your teasing," she said, good-naturedly. "You didn't remember where our campsite had been. I had trouble believing this pile of rubble was what you sought. It resembled many you passed up getting here. I didn't want to say anything. But I'll get you back for your tease."

"So skeptical, my dear friend." Angel laughed heartily. Serylda joined in the good humor before both girls turned serious. "Actually, my crystal is sensitive to the Centauri inside, becoming very warm to my skin. That's how I knew for sure."

Serylda cleared the last of the rubble away and gestured. "You lead."

They proceeded a few yards when Angel sensed the dwarf's uneasiness concerning the darkness and stopped. It surprised her knowing Serylda grew up in the caverns of Jasper. And she had said earlier she couldn't wait to see the caverns. Perhaps Serylda's uneasiness came from the darkness of the passage they found themselves, whereas Jasper's halls were always well-lit. Retrieving a lamp from her pack and lighting it, she continued, the passage now illuminated. Angel proceeded confidently because she knew the floors were smooth and free of obstacles.

"I had no idea the passage would be so narrow," Serylda whispered. "I'm glad I'm not squeamish about such matters."

Very gently Angel probed her friend's mind. The dwarf harbored no fear, but something made her uneasy. Angel decided not to invade deeper into her mind to find out the reason for the uneasiness. She knew the apprehension usually put a dwarf into a form of battle mode. *Not good in here,* she thought.

Aloud, she said, "I guess living inside caves makes one better able to cope with such a problem, huh?" In a joking fashion to try and ease Serylda's disquiet, she added, "Why are you whispering? You don't have to, you know. Anyway, you just said you weren't squeamish. So, relax."

"I can't seem to. I don't know why but it feels like I'm inside a burial chamber. This place feels centuries old." She drew in a deep breath and let it out slowly. "I don't know why I feel this way. I hate this feeling. Our caverns are old, too. It's not natural for a dwarf. How much farther do we need to go?"

Angel chuckled. "Not much farther, friend. Remember, I've been in here before. Trust me. You can talk normally, just like in Jasper. Nothing bad will happen. We are all allies in here."

They traveled ten more minutes. Knowing how time seemed to stop in the caverns, Angel recalled her own feelings long ago. The time it had taken her to reach the end of this tunnel had felt like eternity that first occasion. She sympathized with the dwarf. *Perhaps she is feeling the time difference in here,* Angel thought.

"We're almost there," she reassured Serylda, pointing to the boulder at the end of the passage. It sat off to the side, not blocking the entryway into the living area as it had when she first came here. Thinking of the moved boulder, Angel smiled to herself. *Kalika is either waiting for us or they left it like that after Avery and I left them here,* she thought.

They moved into the short passage and came into a medium-sized room. Serylda gasped. Angel followed the dwarf's line of sight. The Centauri still lined the wall as she remembered. Only three more bodies had joined the line. Angel walked over to them. Serylda followed close behind.

"This *is* a burial vault," the dwarf whispered accusingly. "We shouldn't be here."

Angel ignored her and pointed to the two bodies at the end and spoke in a normal voice. "These were the ones I talked to that fateful day. The day my life really changed." The girls stood in reverence a few moments before a male voice broke the silence.

"If you'd shown up a month ago, you could've talked to them."

The girls swung around. Unconsciously, Serylda unsheathed her sword and raised it, ready for a nonexistent battle.

"Easy, Serylda. I didn't mean to alarm you." Former King Iomar Soren stepped from the shadows, a grin on his face. "Welcome home, Angel." He strode toward them with his hands outstretched.

Sheepishly, Serylda sheathed her sword. "Sorry."

Angel gave Iomar a big hug. "It's good to see you again, father. I'm glad you're still with us. You look as if you haven't aged since I last saw you."

"It's these caverns." He gestured around. "I seem to lose myself in here. How long has it been?"

"Thirteen years, sir. And Avery and I have children, twins, a boy and girl, aged eleven."

"Thirteen years, huh? And I'm a grandfather." Iomar shook his head and quietly laughed. "It's amazing how time just slips away in here." He gave Serylda a quick hug which surprised her. Turning, he added, "Let's go find Kalika. She waits for you both."

They followed the old man through a short passage and into another room. This one contained two cozy couches situated in one corner and a stone table near another doorway. Kalika sat at the table smiling. Angel smiled back and reflected upon her surroundings.

"I like what you two have done to this place." Angel turned to Serylda. "The last time I was here, the table was the only furniture in here."

Kalika rose. "Yes. Well, we Centauri don't really need all that comfort."

"I insisted on the furniture." Iomar moved to one of the couches and sat down. "I've lived in comfort too long to not have someplace to sit myself into. You three have things to discuss. If you don't mind, I'm taking a nap." He leaned back, but just as suddenly, he bolted upright.

"Kalika, maybe you should take them outside. You know how time passes in here."

He leaned back again and closed his eyes. Momentarily they heard snoring coming from him. Angel shook her head at how fast the old king fell asleep. She shrugged her shoulders and chuckled at the other women. Kalika shrugged back.

"Before we leave, can you answer a question?" Serylda requested. At Kalika's nod, she continued. "Earlier we had a discussion about the time Angel arrived here. The dwarves in Jasper have hunted for the two Ancient Ones who were responsible for Angel and her sister's arrival. We never found them."

Kalika looked down at her hands a moment before replying. "Angel, remember when you freed Ahriman? He disappeared. Look closely at the Centauri Memorial. I know you recognize the third from the end."

"Yes." Angel thought a moment, then exclaimed, "Oh. The two who brought us here are on that wall, too, right?"

"They are the fourth and fifth, the two on the right of Ahriman. When we die, these caverns call to our bodies. When we landed on your planet, we transformed this cavern system for our essence. No one in your past time ever knew we were here. Since I am the last of my kind, when I die, I will be called here and the caverns will collapse, entombing us forever."

"Thank you for explaining that," Serylda replied. "But, I am ready to leave. I still feel uneasy."

The trip to the surface seemed quicker than it did reaching the living quarters of the Centauri. Again Angel remembered her feelings fifteen years ago and experienced a comfort knowing that it was the same.

"Wait," Serylda frowned. "Why is the sun going down already? We weren't inside the caverns that long."

"That's what the king was trying to convey," Angel said. "There's something about the caverns that tends to slow down time inside. I'm not sure how." She gripped the dwarf's shoulders. "Now you understand my reactions of so long ago." Serylda nodded and Angel let her go. While in contact with the dwarf, Angel felt the uneasiness in Serylda had disappeared.

"More specifically, Angel, it's the Centauri inside that change the time continuum." Kalika found a seat and gestured for the girls to join her. "Now tell me why you think you are here."

Serylda strode to the canyon's rim, too restless to sit. However, Angel sighed and sat down on the boulder near the queen's left side.

Angel knew the queen's deception. Kalika knew why they sought her out. *Well, if she wants me to say it, so be it. I'll humor her.* "It's Stormy," she said aloud. "She's bombed Krikor and may have used a nuclear device. I'm not sure if any of our people escaped. And I don't know what to do now." She buried her face in her hands.

"Stormy must be destroyed," Kalika said quietly but firmly.

Angel straightened up. "I don't think I can do that. I still love my sister, though she's lost her way."

"I could do it," Serylda spoke up. Her voice carried determination, strong and rock hard. Angel sensed the vow she made so long ago, still fresh in her friend's mind, and felt grateful Serylda was her friend, not her enemy.

Kalika stared hard at Angel. "Stormy must be destroyed," she repeated. "You know that is the only way to end this madness. I'm sorry, Angel."

Angel stared at her hands clasped between her knees. "I understand."

"No, you don't, my child. The nuclear bomb you spoke of isn't the only weapon to be concerned about. There is another weapon, more powerful. I learned it from Stormy herself. She sent me a mental image of it when she tried to threaten me years ago. I didn't want to alarm anyone and kept the information to myself. Once again, recently, she's tried to get in touch with me. I was able to discern her plans to use this doomsday weapon, one from my home planet."

Serylda turned and faced the other women. Both girls frowned and listened intently as Kalika continued.

"Originally, it wasn't a weapon. But, Ahriman showed me by thought mode that he had altered this device just before you and your sister arrived. He had hidden it and I thought it remained so. Now, I'm afraid it may have been found and is capable of total destruction of this entire planet's ecosystem."

Angel gasped. Her head jerked up to look at the old queen. "Why would your people have such a device? Something capable of being turned into such a weapon? I thought you were a peaceful people."

"That is still true, Angel. This device was intended to aid us in colonizing a desolate world free of any life. If one wanted to, it could be reconfigured into a weapon. We knew the danger of our technology.

That fear led us to our awakening. We never intended it to be used as a weapon and vowed to die as a species than let that information loose." The old Centauri bowed her head in shame. "I am truly sorry once more for our interference."

"What do you mean?" Serylda interrupted as she sat beside Angel.

"We hoped our presence wouldn't pose a hazard to humans. This device was made for colonization only, as I said. We never learned of its hiding place, though, in secret, we had sent elves out to try and find it. Not until Stormy contacted me and threatened me with it did I learn it had been found." Kalika studied them a moment.

Angel sensed Kalika's mind touching her own. *She's checking our resolve. I hope I'm strong enough to fight this new threat.*

Kalika continued, "You need to find the location of this menace before Stormy has the chance to use it. Before she learns of my location."

Angel looked down at her hands. "Why is it important to find it before she finds you? Why would she be looking for you anyway?"

"It works in only one way." The queen rose and walked to the edge of the shelf. She studied the vast expanse before facing the girls. They looked at her questioningly, waiting patiently for her to continue.

"I need to explain something for you to understand the true danger we face. When you defeated Ahriman by touching his mind, he was able to read your mind, too. He discovered our general vicinity here at the canyon but not the exact location of the caverns. In the process of your defeating the evil entity inside him, the whereabouts of this device was forgotten. Recently, the location has been remembered by the entity in your sister's form." Kalika returned to sit next to Angel.

"You see, Angel. That is why I called you here. I am the one in mortal danger, now. For this weapon to work properly, a live Centauri has to be sacrificed with the weapon. The combination of our DNA and the chemical composition of the device starts the cascading effect and thus, destruction of what it was used on. It takes around sixty of the earth's days for it to do the job."

"Wouldn't the DNA still work if you were dead?"

"No, Angel. There is something in our DNA when we're alive that disappears when we die. This something is the catalyst. This something is also what allows us to move through time.

"Heed my words. If you do not find her, Angel, or at least the bomb, before she finds me, this world is doomed. Stormy is trying to get to

me by destroying my beloved city and forcing me into a confrontation."
Kalika did something that alarmed both girls. She placed her face in her
hands and began weeping. "I'm sorry I can't help you any more than that.
My people have caused so much misery for your planet. I cannot see you
ever forgiving us." The old queen started trembling.

Angel took hold of one of Kalika's hands. "The only thing you're
guilty of is being alive. And we all share that one. You come from such
noble people. It's just as much our fault. Remember, your people arrived
here to help us. I still remember how messed up this world was, polluted
and always on the verge of war. Your people's arrival just gave the rulers
of that time an excuse to go to war. I believe Mother Nature has done a
wonderful job of the clean-up in the years since. Trust me, my queen,
it's not now, nor has it ever been, your fault." She took a deep breath and
let Kalika's hand loose. "Or your people's fault."

"Just one moment, Angel," Serylda interrupted. She stood with her
hands resting on her hips. "How can it not be their fault?" She pointed
at the Centauri. "If they had never arrived here, I believe we wouldn't be
in this fix, and you wouldn't now have to kill your own sister."

"You may not be here, either, my friend." Angel rose and stood beside
Serylda. Both girls turned and faced the great chasm. "I do remember
how bad it was even though I was pretty young. You can't imagine
the diseases we had because of the poisons we dumped recklessly into
the air and oceans. The earth was overcrowded with people, terrorism
abounded, just a lot of killing. I could go on." She placed an arm around
Serylda. "This time and age," and Angel gestured, "is far healthier than
the time I came from. Please, don't blame Kalika, or any of the Centauri,
for the problems we face today. We will handle it. We are strong. Trust
yourself and the ones around you." *As I finally trust myself,* she added
silently.

Serylda huffed and moved a little away from Angel, breaking contact.
"I'm not as forgiving, Angel. Perhaps if I had lived in your time, I'd feel
differently. It's hard to imagine it being so bad."

Angel nodded in understanding. "It was, Serylda."

The dwarf turned and faced the other two. Her conviction
straightened her spine. "I will take your word on this, dwarf friend.
And that is because of the deep friendship we share. You've proven your
worth and honor many times."

"Then, let's sit and think this through. For one thing, how exactly is this device supposed to work?" The girls joined Kalika as they waited for her answer.

"Its original purpose was to sterilize, then fertilize the soil, preparing it to accept the flora and fauna from Centaurus. I won't go into how it's been changed since I don't know how that was accomplished." Kalika rose to quash any questions the girls wanted to ask.

"I can help you in one thing. I have a radiation detector I'll retrieve. It will help you determine if Stormy used a nuclear device on our beloved city. Please don't leave until I return. Time will pass for you. Though for me, it will only be about an hour." She reentered the cave leaving them where they sat.

The girls exchanged looks and shrugged at Kalika's quick retreat. They might as well make camp where they found themselves. They dare not try to climb out. The crescent moon left too little light to be of use. Besides, Serylda had commented, it was setting. Angel nodded her understanding and sent a mental note to Niedra about their delay. The cat told her all was well upside. With darkness having already fallen, they built a small fire near the entrance for warmth. Gathering some leaves they formed a makeshift bed and settled down for the night.

It was midmorning before Kalika returned to the girls. The date was December 23 and the weather was balmy and dry. The girls had spent a reasonably comfortable night near the entrance. Being warmer inside the caverns, the escaping air and fire helped keep the girls warm overnight. The morning found the girls refreshed when the old queen reappeared. In her possession she carried a small box which she handed over to Angel.

"This is a Geiger counter," Kalika explained.

She showed Angel how it worked. Serylda didn't understand the concept and turned to look across the chasm. After teaching Angel the box's workings, she took the box and handed it to Serylda who started the trek to the top. Kalika told Angel what the radiation could do and how to protect from it. In turn, Angel promised the old queen she'd teach others about this threat.

Angel bowed and thanked Kalika. "I shall take my leave of you now. I hope it won't be so long before we meet again, my dear Centauri." She gave Kalika a big hug.

"I have one more thing to tell you," the queen said. "I think you are ready to learn of the ancient evil of the Centauri. I know how curious you've been in learning this truth. We call them the Zaxcellians. It was a Zaxcellian who possessed Ahriman and is now in possession of your sister. Beware of this being when you confront Stormy. In the meantime, if you need my assistance, send me a thought. I will hear it through your crystal and help you if I can."

"Yes, ma'am." Angel gave Kalika one more hug before letting her go. After watching Kalika disappear back into the caverns, she hurried to join Serylda already halfway out of the canyon.

On the way back to Jasper, Angel taught Serylda all she had just learned of the effects of radiation. She demonstrated how the Geiger counter worked and how it revealed the whereabouts of the dangerous rays. By the time Angel had explained everything she knew, Serylda understood fully the danger Stormy may have leashed upon Krikor.

The girls arrived at Jasper thirteen days later. Angel sent a mental greeting to her husband when they were a mile from the caverns. She felt Avery keeping something very important from her. It worried her enough she raced the horses that last mile, reaching the entrance, their mounts a little breathless. They were met on the surface by a tearful Ariel and a healed but somber Avery. Angel dismounted and grabbed the elf girl's shoulders. Before she let herself read it from the girl's mind, she asked, "What's happened?"

"I'm sorry," Ariel whispered. "I've lost the children." And she started crying, her face in her hands.

CHAPTER 4

Questions and Answers

A FTER DISMISSING A CLASS STUDYING the weapons on the walls, acting Dwarflord Barak Blackstone led everyone into Jasper's War Hall. Angel sat Ariel down in the nearest available chair and took the seat to her left. Avery sat on Ariel's other side. Barak strode to the head of the oval table and waited for everyone to settle down before he took to his own seat.

Angel placed the Geiger counter she carried onto the table. She looked up to see Rick hovering behind Ariel and quickly looked away. She accidently sensed his worry and compassion for her. Obviously they had grown close to each other but not in a romantic way. The elf girl mirrored Angel's terror for the children, for her babies. Ariel was terrified for the twins, but especially for Nicholas.

Well, this is a surprise. Trying to keep calm Angel concentrated upon Ariel and not her children, a hard thing to do. *She's in love with Nicholas and doesn't realize it. At least Rick's hands on her shoulders are having a calming effect on her.* Though Angel felt guilty in reading Ariel's mind, she felt that she needed to have a talk with Avery about this new development. But, in the meantime...

"Okay, Ariel, tell us what happened."

"I went to get the twins for supper and they weren't in their rooms." She started crying and hid her face in her hands. "I'm so sorry. It was my fault."

Angel put her hand on the girl's arm. "It wasn't entirely your fault. Remember, they've done this sort of thing before. By the way, where's Nicholas?"

"Looking for them," Rick admitted. "He sent us to let you know what's happened."

"I see." Angel sat back and studied the two of them. "Well, do either of you know where he went to look for the children?"

"Amar," whispered Ariel. She stole a glance at Avery while Angel noted the fear in her eyes.

"What?" Avery interrupted. "You told me you didn't know. I thought I felt deception in you."

"I'm sorry. I didn't want to cause you more worry before Queen Angel arrived. I've messed everything up." Ariel started crying again.

Avery patted the elf girl's shoulder, his compassion returning. "It's okay. I understand your reasoning. I didn't want you thinking your deception went unnoticed." He jumped up and began pacing the room. "But why did they go to Amar?"

"Why don't you tell us what you know," Angel suggested. "And, this time don't leave anything out."

"Three days after you left, I found the twins missing," Ariel began. "So, I went in search of Nicholas..."

—◦◦◦◦◦◦◦—

Ariel found Nicholas leaving the map room. "Have you seen the twins this morning? I went to get them for breakfast, but I can't find them."

"No, sorry," Nicholas said. He noted her agitation. "You're worried. Why?"

"Jamala is missing, too."

Richard Dilmar marched up behind them. "Sir, the cook wanted me to inform you there's meat missing in the kitchen."

He narrowed his eyes and turned with his hands on his hips. "What meat?"

"The dried venison you were going to use on your hunt next week. Also, the stable hand wanted you to know one of the horses is missing."

Nicholas faced Ariel and sighed. "It looks like they've slipped away." He uttered a few curses and dropped his hands to his sides. "They've done it to me again."

Ariel put her face in her hands and started weeping. "What are the king and queen going to say? They trusted me to keep the twins safe."

"Hey, don't worry." Nicholas patted her on her back. "This has happened before, remember? Of course, the last time, it was my fault for believing they had gotten permission to hunt with me. So, I'm just as much at fault. Did you say their cat was missing, too?"

"Yes."

"Then I bet Jamala is with them. And if that is so, she'll take care of them until we find them."

"Do you think we can find them?" Ariel looked up at Nicholas. Hope filled her eyes.

"Sure. To be honest, I'd been expecting this to happen. But not so soon. I'll get some supplies ready. You get what you need and meet us at the front gate." He turned and motioned for Rick to follow him. Everyone knew the other man's tracking skills were legendary. "Come on, my friend. We've two wayward children to find."

"Yes, sir." Rick smiled. His teeth seemed too white for his ruddy complexion.

The three of them met at the front gate an hour later. Ariel had made them each a couple of sandwiches. She didn't want to waste time eating first. They could eat them on the way as their breakfast. Nicholas had gathered enough supplies to last two weeks before they'd be forced to forage. They knew how determined the twins could be. Hopefully they'd find them and be back before their supplies ran low. Besides, they were only a day ahead of them at the most. They piled their supplies onto one of the four horses Rick had led from the stables and immediately set out.

"One thing is in our favor, sir," said Rick. "They took the piebald, the one with the bad shoe."

Even so, they tracked the twins' trail out of the swamp with some difficulty. Rick proved his tracking skills in the marsh. He led on foot as the other two took control of the horses. Rick pointed out the faint traces of the cat and horse to Ariel. Obviously they had Jamala with them. Nicholas was thankful for that. He also noted that the twins were following their parents' trail to Jasper.

Their search dragged on for nearly two weeks, longer than Nicholas expected. The twins traveled faster than he imagined. Still, they were thankful for the good weather. In all that time, they had one day of snow. Rick used every one of his tracking skills to keep them on the vanishing trail. Just before noon on the eleventh day from Damek, they came across subtle signs of a battle. Rick found a half-buried body a little off to the south. He rose after spending a little time examining it.

"That's one of Stormy's men. I wonder what happened here." He studied the traces he found on the ground. "Well, King Fraomar and his group were here. I've found an elfin arrow." He picked it up and handed it to Nicholas.

"I hope no one was hurt," Ariel whispered. She gasped moving her hand to her mouth. "I hope the twins weren't here. Nicholas, what if they were? What if...?"

"Don't go getting yourself upset by coming to conclusions, Ariel," Nicholas said as he examined the arrow closely. "We don't know all that happened here. But, I believe this battle happened before the twins showed up. They weren't witnesses to it."

"I think the twins are okay," Rick interrupted. He held up a used water skin. "It smells of juice, the kind the twins are fond of. I found it over there." He pointed northwest as he remounted his horse. "Their trail goes that way."

They left the battlefield in the direction the twins had taken. Rick led the way. About two hours later they came across a campfire. They dismounted and handed Ariel their reins. Rick concentrated his skills on the numerous tracks surrounding them. After studying the campfire a few minutes, Nicholas concluded it was only a day old. The twins were close.

"I'm amazed how fast the twins have been traveling," Nicholas commented. "I thought we'd have caught up with the two by now."

"The trail is different," Rick said. "There's more tracks. And I've lost Jamala's and the horse's tracks."

"You're right," Nicholas agreed. "Look around, both of you. See if you can find any trace of Jamala. Forget about the horse."

Ariel found the cat's prints going off toward the north. "Nicholas, over here."

"She was following something," Rick said, puzzled.

"Yes, but not the twins. I wonder why." Nicholas frowned.

"Wait," Rick said a moment later. "I've found their trail. Jamala was following the twins but out away from the main trail. Smart cat."

"You're right. Come on." Nicholas and Ariel remounted while Rick stayed on the ground and kept his eyes on the cat's faint prints.

They found the cat near death a mile down the trail. After examining the cat, Ariel informed them someone had poisoned her. She gave the animal some herbs and waited. The cat expelled what she had in her stomach a moment later. Ariel gave Jamala different herbs to help her with what poison she had already absorbed into her system.

"Will she recover?" Nicholas asked, leaning over both of them.

"I'll know in about half an hour," Ariel said. She sat next to the big cat. "I don't want to move her just yet, so we may as well eat something."

Rick found some berries still on a vine. As they ate, Ariel kept a quiet watch on the cat. The men sat a little away from Ariel and Jamala, quietly talking to themselves. Rick acted very afraid of the animal. Nicholas couldn't resist teasing him about it.

"I never could get close enough to any animal to befriend them. Except a horse, of course. And," he pointed, "*that* is a badgercat. I don't care how much ribbing you give me, Nicholas."

A little more than the thirty minutes that Ariel had predicted Jamala lifted her head and quietly mewed.

Ariel gave a sigh of relief. "I think she'll be fine. But she needs to be carried."

"Well, don't look at me. As I've already told you, I'm not getting close to that cat." Rick held up his hands and backed away.

"Don't worry," Ariel interjected. "She seems to know what's happening."

"It won't be too hard to make a sling for her," Nicholas said.

Using some rope Nicholas and Rick fashioned a rough hammock between two branches. They took two blankets and made a bed on the hammock before attaching the sling to Ariel's horse. Rick faced his fear and helped Nicholas pick up the cat and place her onto the sling. It took both men to accomplish the feat. As they lifted the cat, they noticed the animal didn't fuss, still too sick.

Nicholas, a smile on his face for his friend, couldn't help but say, "I'm sure glad Jamala isn't fully grown."

"Yeah," Rick agreed. "They don't reach their full size until they're two, right?"

"Yes," Nicholas answered, and laughed. "You can relax, my friend. She looks pretty comfortable in that sling."

Ariel positioned herself on her horse and looked back at the cat. The men mounted their horses after assuring themselves Ariel was ready.

"Which way?" Nicholas asked.

"The trail leads to Amar. I suggest we start there," Rick suggested.

The cat gave a feeble meow.

"I think she agrees," said Ariel.

"Then to Amar we go," Nicholas decided.

They traveled northward for eleven days. Jamala felt well enough to walk on her own after the third day. They were about two hundred miles from Amar. Feeling anxious and a little afraid for the twins, Nicholas called a halt. It was taking too long to reach the sinister city. He sent Rick and Ariel to Jasper for help. Jamala refused to go with them, so, Nicholas allowed her to stay with him.

—⁓⊙⊱⊙⊰⊙⊱⊙⊰⊙⁓—

"And so, he ordered me to escort Ariel back here and inform you of his plans," Rick finished. "We learned we arrived here hours after you passed by on your way to the Great Crack."

"I decided you needed to see Kalika more than worry about the twins," Avery confessed. "Besides, Rick and Ariel arrived here before me."

"It was my idea to wait until you both were here to tell you the whole story," Ariel added. "It's all my fault." Again, Ariel buried her face in her hands and sobbed.

Angel sighed deeply. "Girl, you again forget how willful the kids can be. I want you to stop blaming yourself."

Ariel turned a teary face to Angel.

"Remember, we disciplined them for going fishing with Nicholas without telling us."

"Yes. I felt so sorry for them."

"I know. And they had promised to never do that again. They've broken their promise, not you."

"I understand." Ariel wiped her tears away and awkwardly smiled at Angel.

"That's better," Angel said, smiling back before becoming serious. "Now, we need to decide what to do. Avery?"

"We may need help if they're in Amar. We may have a fight on our hands in order to get them back." Avery leaned forward, sighed, and covered his face with his hands.

"You're right, my friend," Barak said. "My coronation has been moved to early tomorrow morning. Avery and I have readied supplies and troops awaiting your return, Angel. We just didn't know where we were headed. After I'm officially crowned Dwarflord, we'll go after your children. You remember General Mandek, I presume." Angel nodded, amazed the old dwarf was still alive. Barak continued, "This is usually not done but I'm placing him in charge and coming with you. He'll close Jasper's doors if Stormy sends her army this way. I have complete confidence in him protecting Jasper. And that leaves me free to aid you. So, I'm going to change the subject. What is this box you've placed on my table?" He gestured.

"Queen Kalika gave me this to aid us in determining the extent of damage at Krikor." Angel opened the box and took out the contraption. She tried explaining the hazards of radiation and how the Geiger counter detected it. She had no luck. *I wish Kalika had joined us here,* she thought, frustrated. *She knows these people better than I, even after fifteen years. Perhaps she could've explained this better. Still, I wonder how much my problem with explaining this is due to my concern for the children.*

"What was that word again? Radiation?" Cornellius's question broke her musings.

Angel sighed. Everyone seemed to be having a hard time with the word. Well, she never passed herself off as a teacher. What she needed was a piece of radioactive rock. Maybe just turning the contraption on like Kalika did for her would help. She took the chance. The Geiger counter clicked sporadically.

"Do you hear that?" Angel looked at each person in the room. "That is saying there's a very little bit of radiation in here."

"Doesn't that mean we're in danger?" Serylda asked in alarm. At least she grasped the new concept better than the others. Angel had to remind herself this was the dwarf's second time to hear this.

Angel chuckled. "No. That is background radiation. It's everywhere, a natural process of decomposition of certain rocks." With the exception of Serylda and Rick, no one seemed to understand. She wondered about Nicholas and wished he was there being the same age as Rick. Perhaps she was just using too many unfamiliar words.

She sighed. "Look, why don't you just trust me. I don't have the words needed to explain it. Queen Kalika gave it to me, remember that."

Everyone nodded and accepted her assurance.

She yawned. "Sorry. I feel so tired; although, I don't think I could sleep with my children in jeopardy. I wish we could leave now."

Avery rose. "I think we're all tired. It'll be easier for everyone if we try to sleep on it."

Barak agreed. "My coronation comes early enough. We can come back here after the ceremony, when we'll still be refreshed, to finalize our plans." He dismissed the gathering, and staying in the war room, closed the door after everyone left.

Avery led a tired Angel to a small apartment he'd been using. Being near Barak's quarters, they would hear anything firsthand, if by chance, Nicholas and the twins appear.

"Let's try to rest," Avery was saying. He sat on the couch.

Since she no longer had to keep up the pretense of being in control, Angel began pacing the moment they entered the apartment. Her babies were possibly in Amar, a fact which scared her like nothing else ever had. Feeling helpless and in a near panic, she turned toward her husband silently begging for strength as a tear escaped her eye.

Avery patted the seat beside him. "Come and relax. We can't do anything right now. If Nicholas finds them, they'll be fine. We just have to hope he does. I feel your anxiety. Know this, beloved, I'm as worried as you."

"I feel I've let them down. I don't think I can cope with this, Avery." She moved over to him and sat down. "I have so much fear inside me for them. It's worse than my confrontation with Ahriman." She put her head on his shoulder and allowed another tear to escape.

He placed a comforting arm around her. "Jamala is with Nicholas. We know how protective she can be with the children. Have comfort in that."

She looked up at him. "I know you don't believe that any more than I do. But," and she smiled at him, "I'll try to be as strong as you, my love."

They rose as one and retired. Their bodies were exhausted though they knew neither of them would sleep well that night.

The coronation of Barak Blackstone went quickly the next morning. The entire population of Jasper remained solemn and the ceremony lasted no more than five minutes. Angel knew Ganesh Blackstone was loved by many and would be sorely missed.

After the ceremony, Barak informed his subjects of the lost children. He told them to obey General Mandek in his place so he could aid the elf queen and king in their search. The people gave their new dwarflord an enthusiastic "good luck" as he turned away.

Back in the war room, discussions were underway among eight persons. There were the elves: Avery, Angel, and Ariel. Cornellius and Rick sat in for the men of Damek. And for the dwarves, there was the newly made dwarflord, Barak with his sister Serylda and General Mandek.

"I have seventy dwarves ready for battle, sire," said the general.

"Good," Barak acknowledged. "We can use the horses to carry our supplies. It should take about two weeks to reach Amar."

"No," Angel interrupted, her emotions barely in control. "That's too long, Barak. I can't do that."

Why don't we take the horses and let the army follow?" Rick asked. "There's eight of them in the stables."

"That's a good idea," Avery said. "We can see what we're getting into before the army arrives. It may delay a fight, or even keep one from happening."

"That sounds better to me, Barak," Angel said, silently imploring him to heed her.

Barak thought a moment. "Well, it does sound a faster way to get there. Though I hate riding on those animals. Does everyone agree with it?" With nods from all present and a grateful sigh from Angel, Barak continued. "Very well. General Mandek, I trust you to defend Jasper if needed." At the general's nod, Barak glanced once more at the faces surrounding him. "I guess we're ready, then. I call this short meeting closed. I'll meet with you outside after I let Morna know of our plans."

Sunshine and a slight breeze greeted them outside lower Jasper. For January 6, it proved optimistic. The temperature was mild and a few clouds played in the sky. The seventy dwarves General Mandek had promised began their march as Angel and the others waited for Barak.

Meanwhile, Angel whistled for Niedra. The confines of the caverns made the big cat nervous so she had stayed outside to hunt and stretch out. The others saddled the horses and led them to the entrance to await the dwarves. Shortly, Barak, clasping hands with Morna, arrived with Serylda and General Mandek in tow.

"Keep the place safe until we return, my old friend," Barak said.

"Don't worry, sire." The general exchanged a strong handshake with Barak. "I will guard your kingdom with my life."

With an uncharacteristic gesture, Barak grabbed Morna and kissed her soundly in front of the crowd. No one whooped to see the unusual display from him. They understood the seriousness of the situation. After a few minutes of holding her tight he passed her to General Mandek.

"She's the most important person, Mandek."

"Of course, sire," the general agreed. He bowed low and gently tucked Morna under his arm in a grandfatherly gesture. She allowed the familiarity with her head held high.

The seven mounted their horses. Angel turned to look back at the general and Morna. She noticed the arm around her comforted Morna a little. *She's so worried but taking it like a soldier,* Angel thought, curiously moved. *I can learn from her how to control my own emotions. Even so, I swear I will bring her husband back safely.*

The seven passed the dwarf army a short time later and left them behind. The night was clear and cool when they stopped and made their first camp. The moon being past full wouldn't be up for another hour. They enjoyed some rabbit Cornellius's two falcons caught. Ariel, the group's cook, roasted the meat over the fire and boiled some vegetables to round out their meal. To finish the meal, Barak made his famous coffee for everyone to enjoy. With filled mugs in hand, they relaxed around the fire.

"Barak, how long do you think it'll take to get to Amar?" Angel asked.

"About one week, half the time it'd taken us on foot."

"Can't we get there any faster?"

"Not without overtiring the horses," Cornellius answered her.

"Angel, why don't you tell us what you found out at the Great Crack?" Avery suggested. "We haven't had time to hear your story. Besides, it'll take all our minds off the children for a short time."

Angel regarded her friends surrounding her. They all watched her intently, waiting for her to say anything.

She sighed before saying, "I have to destroy Stormy."

They waited for more.

"That's all?" Avery prompted.

"What else can I say? I have to kill my own sister. Isn't that enough?" Angel laid a comforting hand on Niedra's big head when she growled.

"She feels my pain. Don't worry about her," Angel added. She felt the tension harbored in Barak when the cat made a sound. "As you all know, she won't hurt anyone. She's just showing her concern."

"Yes, well." Barak exhaled sharply. He sipped his coffee and glared at her. "It's time you explained how it is you found Queen Kalika, at her age, alive and well at the Great Crack among the Ancient Ones. Everyone assumed she'd be dead by now."

Angel studied each person surrounding her over her coffee mug. She held everyone's attention, more so after Barak's inquiry. She took a big gulp of her now warm coffee and lowered her mug. *Yes*, she thought, *I need to tell them the Centauri secret. I no longer need to worry over this moment.*

"You're right, Barak. There is a truth you need to know. The Elven Nation is made up of the seed of man and one Centauri, the beings you know as the Ancient Ones. Queen Kalika is over two thousand years old. She was the youngest of the Centauri who arrived on this planet so long ago."

Angel didn't have to look at her audience to know that only the elves weren't shocked. When Angel became queen, Kalika decided to tell her people the truth. Since it was an elfin matter, no one else in the world needed to know. All this time, they had been communicating with one of the Ancient Ones and had no idea. Angel, knowing how much a surprise it became to the others, took a drink of her coffee to allow them to digest the information.

"When Ahriman had caused the Third World War, the remaining Centauri devised a plan to correct this mistake. Many people died in the devastation. Fear arose that the races of Man and Centauri were on the brink of extinction. They selected the youngest and healthiest among themselves to assist in the continuation of both species. Kalika became the queen. Several men, women, and children followed her to a safe haven. With Kalika's help, this new colony built what you now know as Krikor."

"I would never have guessed that this was Queen Kalika," Rick stated, dumbfounded.

Angel nodded. "Through the years, she had children. They grew up looking as the elves do today."

"Why didn't we know this? Why was it kept a secret?" Barak asked, confused. "And since they kept this a secret, did they cause the dwarves to be who we are today, also? As you know, we always believed we came from the Ancient Ones' working class, not the Ancient Ones themselves, that we were their special children."

"What you say is true, Barak. They decided to let the dwarves keep their belief. You never developed the ears like the elves did. Basically you still look like the human races. But, for the Elven Nation, the Centauri thought it best if the elf beginnings were forgotten. They felt it important that the race of Man be true to their world. They didn't want to start a colony on a world already populated. It was bad enough to have to use their working-class. Time passed and the elves came out of hiding after they forgot their own beginning. Queen Kalika brought about her people's forgetfulness. She pretended to age and die, then come back as a new queen. Tradition argued the new queen was to be named Kalika with an elaborate ceremony. In this way, she kept the secret from becoming known."

"And how did she pretend to age and die and no one discover the truth?" Rick asked.

Angel finished her coffee and set her now empty mug on the ground next to her. "Like I mentioned before, Kalika and her consort would have children. When they grew up and had children of their own, one of the girls would be chosen to become the next queen. She was trained from the time she was three. When she turned twenty-one, she chose her own consort. The people believed them to become the next king and queen. The people never knew that would not be the case. Remember, the only ones knowledgeable about the truth were the old king and Kalika. The ceremony required a trip to the Great Crack. A few elves were allowed to accompany the future royal couple. Queen Kalika and her old consort joined the company."

"We never knew of this ceremony where they traveled passed Jasper," Barak said. "I remember Father talking about once seeing a group of elves traveling west when he was but a boy. They weren't seen returning to the east and was thought to have died. This explains what my father witnessed."

Barak rose and retrieved the coffee pot. He refilled everyone's mugs and sat back down. Angel waited for him to finish before continuing her narration.

"At the Great Crack, only five people were allowed inside. They were Queen Kalika and the old king, the future queen and king, and a young male aide who had grown close to Kalika. Inside, Kalika revealed the truth behind the elves' ancestry. Also, this was when the young future king and queen learned they were staying inside the caverns temporarily. They accepted their destiny, while the aide learned he was to become the new king. Inside the cavern, Kalika transformed back into her younger appearance. The now new Royal Couple would exit the caverns and return to the top of the Great Crack."

"And this would be Kalika and the young aide?" Cornellius asked.

"Yes," Angel answered. "It was the now young-looking Kalika and her new husband who led the people back to Krikor."

"You'd said the young couple stayed in the caverns temporarily. What eventually happened to them?" asked Barak.

Avery answered Barak's question. "There is an elfin haven called Kaliborn. It's located on the northwest coast and has been kept secret since the beginnings of our nation. Only the Royal Couple ever knew the location. Since Angel and I have inherited the throne from Kalika, the secret was revealed to the elves. I can show you the approximate area if you would get a map, Barak."

While Barak rummaged in his backpack, everyone else cleaned their mugs and put them away. All returned to the fire when Barak retraced his steps to his seat. He spread out the map in front of the fire, being careful of the flames.

Avery pointed out the location of Kaliborn. Angel knew it lay someplace near where she remembered the giant redwood trees of California lay of her past time. She wondered if any still stood.

"Are there elves living in Kaliborn today?" asked Barak. "And if so, why haven't we heard from them before now?"

"We hope Kaliborn is populated today," Avery answered. He thought a moment. "We could use their help. If there is a living community, they know of us. Each time the trip was taken, the three newcomers were charged to enlighten the inhabitants of the happenings here. Since my parents left for the Great Crack and Kalika is a Centauri, we've decided to leave them alone for now. We plan to make a trip at a later date. We'll let you know when we do."

"It would be interesting to know," Ariel added. "I've wondered if anyone lives in Kaliborn ever since we were told the story fifteen years ago."

"I agree," said Avery. "There was a reason we were kept in the dark. It was vital we stayed true to this earth and forget we were part Centauri. Now that everyone has been informed of this, we should plan that trip after we fix our immediate problems."

Barak nodded in sudden understanding. "So, Kalika was the chosen one. I think I know why. Someone had to start the legend and make sure it was never forgotten. And as you've told us, since she was the youngest, they chose her."

"True," Angel said. "The religious class had kept a secret from their own people. Certain Centauri had a unique ability to travel through time. As you all know, they felt they made a great mess of things and thought someone from this world's past could correct it; that is, if they didn't accomplish the feat before the legend came to pass. Only seven Centauri remained when they decided upon this action."

"Eight, my dear," Avery interrupted. "Don't forget Ahriman."

"Of course." Angel shook her head and studied her audience a moment. "Well, four Centauri went into the past and brought my sister and myself to their time, with two dying in the process. They never revealed that time to me. They took a drop of my blood and placed it on this crystal." She touched the now famous trinket that never left her neck.

"Kalika was chosen at that time to save man and start the legend. In order to give them time to fix their problem, two other Centauri, their leader and one other, sacrificed their lives to bring us as far into the future as possible. By the way, their leader was Ahriman's father. This was done to allow the two remaining Centauri to do battle with Ahriman. Kalika led a few humans to a safe haven until Ahriman was sufficiently defeated to be of little danger. We now know that sanctuary to be Kaliborn."

"But they didn't defeat Ahriman," Rick added.

"You're right," Angel agreed. "The two Centauri survived the skirmishes with Ahriman and retreated to the Great Crack. When Ahriman was of little danger and Kalika was able to return, she and her followers founded Krikor and began the Alastrine Legend to prepare everyone for my appearance."

"And you did defeat our greatest enemy," Barak added.

Angel sighed. "I should've destroyed him."

"I think you kind of did that, ma'am," Rick said, bowing.

"Yes," Avery said. "He was destroyed and Stormy took his place."

"Yes," she said quietly. "Now I have to destroy her, my sister. That is my dilemma. I really don't think I can do it."

"Well," Serylda interrupted, "I once swore to you I'd kill Stormy for killing my betrothed. You know I still stand by that vow."

"Thank you for explaining the elfin secret to us," Barak said. "Now, do you know anything more of how the dwarves became as we are?"

"I learned from Kalika the Centauri did have a working class that came here with them. Six survived the last confrontation with Ahriman. They escaped underground with some humans who were sympathetic with their plight. These were your ancestors. They reproduced fast and at one point in time, half of the dwarf nation left and formed the Boman colony."

"So, only the Falconlanders are true humans?" Rick asked.

"I'm afraid so."

Everyone fell quiet for a time, digesting all they learned from the current queen and king of Krikor. Not invading her friends' private thoughts, Angel sensed the disbelief turning into conviction. That felt good. They still relied on her trust. Thankful, she didn't let on how big the earth really was. They had enough information, all they needed for now.

Barak rose. "I guess we should get some rest. We still have a long way to go."

"Yes, the twins need to be found before we can deal with Stormy," said Cornellius.

Ariel sighed and looked down. "I should've paid better attention to the children." She let escape a small sob.

Angel put an arm around the elf's shoulder and led her to their tent. "It'll turn out okay. Let's not use up unnecessary energy doubting ourselves."

Serylda followed and the women left the men to tend the fire.

Niedra watched the camp that night. Jasper lay only a days' march from their location. Sentry duty would be set tomorrow and for the days that followed.

Angel thought about all the words said that night. She couldn't help but worry on her children's safety. On top of that, her sister was once more in her thoughts. Somehow she had to save all three. But, would they accept her sister if she accomplished what she set out to do? Would

Serylda, if Stormy was saved and became Alison once again? She prayed she wouldn't have to kill Stormy to save her children. That was the one evil thing she knew she would do. Her children came first.

She let a tear escape. *I wish you could've given me some advice in this, Kalika,* she thought as sleep finally found her.

CHAPTER 5

Nicholas

THREE DAYS PASSED. THEY FOUND themselves halfway to Amar. The November 18 battle site was located nearly four hundred miles southeast of their location. Angel tried not to think of that tragic day. Instead she concentrated on their surroundings. Dense trees encircled them, the kind the twins loved. Their leaves carpeted the forest floor. She looked up. Even with the trees dormant in their winter coats, the numerous branches revealed the clear sky in only a few places. Good weather followed them since leaving Jasper on the twenty-second. Avery informed her earlier he sensed the weather would turn bad tonight or tomorrow. Thankfully Barak chose a secluded site for their camp.

Suddenly she realized she had forgotten Christmas entirely by two weeks! Oh, where were her children? Were they okay? She always enjoyed this time of year with them. But for the first time, her family had missed this joyous season. Depression threatened to weigh her down. *We'll find them,* she told herself. *We have to. And I need to be strong for everyone's sake.*

To keep herself from worrying, Angel walked over to the other women and began helping to set up camp. Serylda and Ariel had the tent laid out, ready to raise. With the poles in place, they raised the tent, then pegged and tied it down. Angel left to gather wood for the night's fire. Serylda finished setting up inside the tent. Ariel helped Rick lay a ring of rocks for the armload of wood Angel handed him.

"Thanks," he said as he accepted her bundle.

"He wanted to cook tonight," Ariel said. She sat down on a nearby log. "That is, if the hunters find us some meat."

"Well," Angel replied with a smile, "I do hope they bring back a rabbit or two. I'm hungry for your famous stew."

Rick laughed and busied himself with the fire. Angel joined Ariel on the log and visited with the two while they waited for the hunters to return.

Darkness had descended by the time the falcons returned and landed on a tree near the fire pit. Angel smiled when she eyed the four rabbits the hunters carried. Ariel volunteered to ready the meat. Before she started dressing the rabbits, the company heard snarls coming from different areas in the surrounding brush.

"Badgercats," whispered Barak. "A group of about four by the sounds of it. Ready your weapons."

Angel held up one arm, suddenly sensing the cats. "Wait. Nobody move." She sensed Niedra nearby. *Help us, Niedra. We're surrounded by your kind.*

I am here. All okay. Five badgercats entered the camp, Niedra in the lead.

"Check it out, Barak." Angel lowered her arm. "You can relax. Niedra has them under her control."

"How sure are you? Those are wild cats, even though Niedra is with them."

"Yes, and she just informed me they are her siblings. They obey her since she is the oldest."

"Can you make sure for my sake?"

Angel nodded and turned to Niedra. *Will they hear me?*

Yes.

Angel turned to the four cats sitting behind her pet. *Do you hear me?*

She heard four distinct voices in her head. One decided to talk for the other three.

I am Seth, the second born. I will talk for us.

Seth, will you harm any of us?

No, my sister said I will die if I do. We will all die.

Angel's eyebrows disappeared into her hair. *Okay. What do you four plan?*

We want to join you.

Angel grunted amusement. *I accept your proposal. One question. How do you know our language so well?*

We have been following you since you first passed us near here. We learned your language from you.

You do not act like other badgercats.

No. Are you mad?

Definitely not, my new friend. I am just astonished. My companions are afraid of your kind.

We know. I hear Barak's voice in my head. I have not answered him. I know what happened to him when he was young. One of us hears another in her head. We all hear yours. This is a confusion for us. We thought you could help.

I am sorry, Seth. I don't know the answer. We need to talk to someone who is more familiar in this. Angel sighed. *Perhaps when we finish our task, we will all go back to what we call the Great Crack.*

We know of it.

We will ask the Centauri still alive in there.

A "Thank you" came from each cat. Then Seth thought to Angel, *We will help you in your quest if you will let us.*

Angel laughed and spreading her hands wide addressed her comrades. "Can you believe this? We have an army of badgercats at our disposal. We are very lucky. Oh, and Rick? Ariel? You two have a ready-made disposal unit for those rabbit bones."

Slowly Rick shook his head. "Amazing. If I hadn't seen this with my own eyes, I wouldn't have believed it. I think I understand a little of what you felt the first time Niedra joined you."

"Not so fast," Barak interrupted. "We may be used to Niedra. But we have four more in our presence now. Have you ever seen what they can do? How fast they are when they rip you to shreds?"

"No, sir."

"I witnessed such a thing in my youth."

"He was the only survivor of a group of four," Serylda explained. "Luck took Barak's side. He survived only because there were three cats and he was farthest away when they attacked."

Rick shuddered. "I hope we have enough bones to satisfy them. I'd hate to wake up as their dinner."

Angel smiled at his apprehension. "Don't worry." She laid a hand on Rick's shoulder. "They are friendly to us. I can talk to them and control them."

Rick, still skeptical after what he'd just learned from the dwarves, glanced at each of his companions. "Can she do that?"

Avery chortled. "Yes. I believe in her. You can, too."

Rick returned to his cooking. Even so, he kept himself between Ariel and the new cats. Ariel, seemingly more comfortable with the animals, stripped the meat and threw the bones to the cats. Rick maintained a watch as they ate.

Barak sighed. "It's a different world," he said, allowing a little amazement to color his voice. He looked sideways at Angel. "Rest assured, I don't feel the intense fear and hatred I harbored at the sight of badgercats. Though I still feel apprehension, it no longer controls me. I owe this sense of peace to you, Angel. Thank you." He bowed low.

She accepted his compliment with a smile. She turned, and since they were finished with gnawing the bones, she tested each new cat. She ordered them to sit in front of her. She checked each cat's emotional states and learned they were as loyal to her as Niedra. She sighed and relaxed.

The company had a very restful night with full bellies and knowing badgercats kept a close vigil.

The next morning they set out with the five badgercats in the lead. The predicted bad weather had waited one more night. The skies carried clouds full of moisture while a chill in the air promised snow.

Twenty miles later, Seth padded up to Angel and asked, *do you think it is safe for me to talk to Barak? I feel close to him but am afraid of his fear for my kind. I very much want to be his.*

Angel looked at the cat, its head even with her own. *Let me say something to him first.*

Will you do that now?

Angel smirked. The poor cat nearly begged her. *I'll say something to him tonight.*

The cat thanked her and padded on ahead. Though she was used to Niedra, Seth was nearly half as much larger. Angel knew the big cat's mind and was glad of that fact. He was very loyal to Niedra, and so was loyal to Angel. In fact, all five were loyal to her.

Suddenly the cats growled softly. Angel spotted a rundown shack ahead. The company readied their weapons and slowly crept up to the shack. Suddenly, Niedra screeched and sent shivers up everyone's back.

"Whoa," Rick said solemnly.

"She's found Nicholas," Angel informed all.

Niedra and Seth stood near the unconscious man behind the shack. The other three cats continued to reconnoiter the area. Angel sent her thanks to the two as she began to check Nicholas. She found no wounds to account for his unconscious state. She sent Seth to watch with his three siblings. Niedra stayed with Angel.

She stood. "I believe he's been poisoned."

Barak and Avery picked up Nicholas and carried him into the shack. The darkening clouds spitted snow at them and the shack was a better place than out in the weather. The men laid Nicholas on the floor next to the fire pit in the center of the room. Meanwhile, Ariel eagerly gathered the herbs needed to help the sick man. After taking the two blankets Rick handed her, Angel sent him to help Ariel. She covered the man with one blanket and used the other for a pillow.

He stirred.

"Shh, my friend," she consoled. "You'll feel better soon."

"Where's the twins?" Nicholas rasped. He tried getting up but Angel held him back while Avery knelt beside him.

"Easy, man. We'll find them. Can you tell us what happened?"

Angel rose. "Not now, Avery. I want to know as badly as you. But first we need to get those herbs inside him to absorb the poison in his system and help him regain his strength. You can help by fetching water for Nicholas to drink and to boil."

Avery nodded and rose. Barak worked on a fire as Avery found a metal pot and filled it with water. Angel gave the sick man a drink then Avery placed the pot with the remainder of water on the fire to boil. At that moment, one of the cats screeched. Angel rose and appeared to be in a trance.

"They've found Jamala," she said.

Leaving Avery with Nicholas, Angel took Serylda and Barak to see where Jamala rested, looking deathly ill. She turned and thanked the cat that found her. The cat mewed back and wandered off. Leaning over the cat, Angel checked Jamala, then rose.

"She's been poisoned, too. Let's get her inside with Nicholas. I can treat her with the same herbs."

Surprising Angel, Barak reached down and gently picked up the big cat, cradling it over his broad shoulder. Nearly too much animal for him, still he carried the sick beast inside and gently laid it down next to Nicholas. Ariel and Rick entered the shack with the herbs Angel needed. She put the herbs in the now boiling water and took the pot off the fire. After allowing it to steep for five minutes, she made Nicholas and Jamala drink some of the concoction. Both were too sick to put up much of a fuss, for which Angel was thankful. She had no way to sweeten the bitter medicine.

Three hours later, Nicholas sat up. Angel checked him over and decided he seemed lucid to her.

"If you begin to feel sick, you let me know."

"Yes, ma'am," he croaked.

Shaking a finger at him she warned, "I want no heroics, Nicholas."

"Yes, ma'am," he repeated with a smile.

Angel made him lie back down before she called out to Avery. He came inside covered in snow. The others followed him inside, all looked dry. Angel raised her eyebrows at her spouse.

He glanced at his clothes and back up at her. "I was pacing."

"Well, I think Nicholas is well enough to talk. Try not to tax his strength."

"Understood," he said as he sat next to Nicholas. "Well, my friend, are you well enough to tell us what happened? And go slowly. We have the time. It's snowing heavily, too hard to see."

"Ariel told us the happenings up to when you sent her and Rick to Jasper," Angel said. "Why don't you start from there?"

Nicholas nodded and began.

"Jamala wouldn't go with Ariel and Rick, so I allowed her to stay with me..."

———w•෨ᐉᚖᚖᐉᚖᚖᐉᚖ•w———

"She'll help me find the kids. Avery and Angel need to know what happened. I'm sending you two to do that."

Although Ariel didn't agree, she obeyed. They parted company. Ariel and Rick headed west while Nicholas and Jamala traveled north.

The weather remained fair during the eight-day trek north. About two hours before sunset, Nicholas and Jamala arrived at the outskirts of Amar, a city full of cutthroats and thieves. He hoped the cat had been wrong about the twins being in this sinister city. He made the cat hide outside the city limits with his horse. She cried at him but acted like she understood his reasons. Being a badgercat she didn't belong in there. Someone would kill her if she entered. They both knew this. Besides Jamala had to watch the horse. He dare not lose it so far from help.

Nicholas wandered through the town. He entered several taverns listening closely to the conversations around him. He got lucky and overheard someone talking about a couple of new young and feisty slaves in a tavern on the north side of town. They could be the twins.

Shortly before sundown the skies turned cloudy. It began sprinkling when he found the tavern and entered. The room grew deathly quiet but soon became noisy again. It took his eyes a few moments to adjust to the gloom. He found himself in a large dark room filled with swarthy cigar-smoking men and a few crude and rowdy women. Each table bore a squat lit candle. In the center of the room a fire burned in a round pit built into the floor. It put out as much smoke as it did heat. Combined with the cigar smoke, the place was too stuffy for Nicholas's taste.

He took a seat on the far side of the room and spotted Janna almost immediately. He sighed at the luck in finding them with little trouble. She was waiting tables in a very skimpy outfit. He spotted Jared in back washing dishes beyond the swinging doors Janna disappeared through.

She returned with a tray of food, deposited it at a nearby table and strode up to his table. "Can I get you anything, sir?"

He allowed a smile to show on his face for a brief moment, then, with a rough voice, asked, "How much for your rooms?"

She winked at him to let him know she was glad to see him. Acting cool, she answered, "We have rooms for fifty tokens. We're the cheapest in town."

"Good. I'll take one. That is if you have one available at the end of a hall. I hate neighbors."

"Yes, sir. I'll see what I can do. In the meantime, would you care for a drink or something to eat?"

"I just want the room."

"Very good, sir. I'll be right back." She left and returned a minute later. "We have one, sir. My master says it's a little more, though. It'll cost you sixty tokens."

"That's fine."

"In advance, sir. I'm sorry." She held out a hand for the money.

"No problem. Here." He handed her the amount requested. Reassuringly, their fingers touched. He rose and she led him to his room.

"Are you sure you don't want anything to eat, sir?" she asked as she led him past the mean-looking, jeering barkeep. The barkeep's leer showed a mouth with very few teeth.

"No thanks," he said. Obviously the man thought he owned her so Nicholas played along. He felt the twins were smart enough to get to him later. She led him up the stairs and to the room at the end of the hall. She opened the door and motioned him inside, staying out in the hallway.

"Check-out time is noon, sir. Have a nice evening." She left, closing the door behind her.

He worried the time away. Everything that could go wrong entered his mind. By midnight, he was becoming uneasy. A quiet rap at the door made him jump. He opened it and stood looking at the twins. Jared grinned at Nicholas.

Wasting no time, Nicholas grabbed both children by their arms and pulled them inside. He glanced down the hallway, and seeing nobody, silently closed the door. Reassured that no one saw the kids, he motioned them toward the window. Once there, he tossed a rope down, one end having been tied to the bed nearby.

The rain made the rope slick. Jared nearly lost his grip when he shimmied down first. Cautiously he called to his sister to be careful and helped her on her climb down. They frowned at each other when the rope disappeared back into the window. A few moments later a pack, tied to one end, appeared through the window, and Nicholas, with the other end of the rope tied to his waist, free-climbed down. The twins followed Nicholas into the surrounding brush behind the tavern and they headed south. A mile later, he stopped and gave both kids a bear hug despite the pouring rain.

"You two will be the death of me yet."

"We're sorry, Nicholas," Jared said, his head hanging low.

"We'll behave," Janna added. "We just miss mom and dad."

"So, you decided to skip out on me, huh?" Nicholas shook his head and harrumphed. "I can't seem to stay mad at you two. Come on. Let's get out of here. Jamala will be glad to see you both."

"She's alive?" Janna asked, hope in her voice.

"Yes, thanks to Ariel."

"Is she here, too?" Jared asked. He grabbed Janna's hand in anticipation of the scolding they were due from Ariel.

"No," Nicholas answered. "Ariel and Rick left for Jasper a couple weeks ago for help."

"Boy are we going to be in trouble," they said in unison.

They traveled another two miles when Nicholas quietly whistled and Jamala jumped from the bushes. The horse gave a whinny, glad to see him. The twins laughed despite being hushed by Nicholas. Jamala wore herself out with her antics. He smiled and shook his head. He let them have some time despite the noise. After a few moments he calmed them down. The twins settled themselves atop the horse with Jamala in front of them. Nicholas led the horse away as the rain began to abate.

"We'd better head for Jasper tonight. Your captors will be looking for you and I want to get as far away as possible from here."

He kept the twins ignorant that someone followed them. He hoped that his tracking skills were good enough to lose their pursuers. With the rain softening the ground, he needed to hide the horse's tracks somehow. Gradually he turned the animal into the brush. The horse the twins had taken from Damek's stables would've been handy right now. Too bad it was lost to them. They would have a hard time outmaneuvering the ruffians following them. As they left Amar farther behind, he prayed they'd be the winners in this race.

—⁓⦿⦿⦿⦿⦿⁓—

"I got the children out of Amar easy enough. But we had one problem. The way Jamala was acting, I figured we were being trailed. Sure wish I could talk to them like you, my lady." He paused and took a sip of the water Angel had fetched for him. He kept hold of the mug as he continued.

"After a while, I thought I'd lost them. So we headed toward Jasper when we met up with this old lady a week later. She said she wanted some company and that she had some stew simmering on her stove. We were pretty hungry and it sounded so good we agreed to follow her." He held up a hand when Cornellius opened his mouth. "I know, uncle. I need to be more cautious of strangers, especially around here. I think she may have done something to us. I remember she smelled so good, which was strange since she looked so old. I don't know. Maybe that was how she did it." He shook his head. "Anyway, she brought us to this shack and fed us each a bowl of great smelling stew and warm aromatic bread. It was so good, I ate three helpings. The twins only ate one. I think she must have put poison in the two extra helpings I ate. She gave Jamala a bone to gnaw on. I think she must have poisoned it, too.

"About fifteen minutes later, I felt funny. The old woman laughed and said she was Stormy. She opened the door and two ruffians entered. I believe they were the ones following us. When she removed her outer clothes, I knew she spoke the truth. She told me she had drugged Jamala and myself and that she was taking the twins to her new hideout. She told me where it was with instructions that you were to meet her there, Angel. That was the only way you'd get your children back. I think if I hadn't passed out then, she would have used the two men on me. As it was, I don't know what happened after that. When I woke next, it was dark and I made myself go outside and try to expel what I had left in my stomach. For the past three weeks, I've been melting snow in that pot for water and found a few berries to eat. I don't know what Jamala did in the meantime."

"Jamala seems worse off than you," Cornellius said. "Did she give her more than you?"

"No, Uncle. I think she was still ill from her first poisoning."

Outside Niedra interrupted them with a screech. Angel listened a moment. "One of the other cats have a man cornered in the brush about half a mile south of here. Niedra will lead someone to him."

"Good. I'm anxious to meet him," Barak rasped. "It's snowing too hard for us to find him without your pet, Angel. Everyone can stay warm. Avery and I will fetch him back here."

With a rope in hand, Barak led the way out. After the men left, the girls concentrated on making Nicholas more comfortable. Jamala slept nearby and seemed okay so they didn't disturb the big cat. Leaving Cornellius to sit beside the sick man, the others went outside. One of the wild cats was sitting on the porch. Angel asked if it could help her find certain herbs. The cat mewed its consent and led them away. They returned shortly with different herbs in hand. *Hopefully, these herbs are still potent enough to help the sick gain their strength back*, Angel thought to herself. Well, she could stay optimistic for their sake.

After getting man and beast into a more healing sleep, Angel left the shack. Ariel and Cornellius watched over Nicholas, talking quietly. Half an hour later, Angel looked up at the feeling of hatred coming from the storm. Avery and Barak returned. Avery, full of rage and unable talk, handed her a note.

"It was found near the man," Barak explained. "He was one of Stormy's troops. We were too late to save his life. We left the cats to finish what they had started."

Angel nodded and glanced at her husband. He paced the small room trying to control his rage. She turned her attention to the note.

> "Hey, Sis," Angel read aloud.
>
> "I hope for your sake you get this note in time. I may have given your friend too much poison. Too bad if I killed him. But, I won't lose sleep over it. You've probably guessed by now that I have control of your children. Nice kids, by the way. I sure hate to have to kill them. I will if you don't come to me by January 30. Head south to Natural Bridge Caverns. You do remember where that was, don't you? Tell that company of yours there will be no heroics trying to rescue the kids from me. If you try, I will kill them slowly. In front of you.
>
> "Stormy.
>
> "PS: By the way, I've destroyed your precious city, Krikor. My gift to you. Merry Christmas."

Angel locked eyes with her spouse when she finished reading the note. She felt numb. All emotion inside her seemed to vanish. Stormy had her kids now, threatening to kill them. What did she do to deserve this?

"What's Natural Bridge Caverns?" Rick asked.

"Barak, if you'll bring me one of your maps, I'll point out the area the caverns are at for Rick," Angel said, her voice hard.

Barak nodded and went to the horses in search of one of his many maps. The rest of them entered the shack to await his return.

"We can't do anything tonight," Serylda said. "First, we need to get Nicholas and Jamala well enough to travel."

""I agree," Barak said, hearing Serylda's last sentence as he entered the building. He took his map and laid it out on the floor. Nicholas and Jamala still slept near the fire. Angel studied the map a moment and pointed where she thought the caverns lay.

"I know that area," Rick said. "Cornellius sent four of us there seven years ago. We spent the night watching fires near those caverns and knew evil brewed there."

"I'd heard rumors and knew of the caverns having been there in my youth," Cornellius explained. "So I wanted information and Rick was one who I thought would benefit from the trip."

"So," Barak rasped. "As we feared, she disappeared into those caverns. I always wondered where she ended up." Dwarflord Barak Blackstone looked at each person staring back at him. Then, addressing Angel, he said, "We can wait for my troops to reach us here. We have the time. They should be here in about four more days. Also, that should give Nicholas and Jamala time to heal."

"I agree," Avery said, breaking his silence, finally gaining control of his rage.

"What happened to the man the cats had found?" Angel asked.

"Well, like I said earlier, we were too late to save him. The cat that found him nearly clawed him to death before we arrived." Barak shuddered. "Believe it or not, I yelled at the cat and it stopped mauling the man. Even so, we were too late."

Angel nodded, recalling Barak had mentioned that already. She moved over to stand next to Avery. He put his arm around her and they all went outside. Niedra rose from her sitting position on the porch. As Angel and Avery stepped off the porch with Niedra shadowing, Angel heard Barak stop Serylda from following them.

"Let them be, sister. They need time alone." Both reentered the building. Rick stayed outside.

———

The date was January 14 when the dwarf army arrived. They made their plans and headed for the meeting with Stormy. Nicholas and Jamala were well enough to join them, still feeling the effects of their poisoning and hunger but recovering nicely.

When she began to feel again, Angel thought she would go insane. She had fretted the time waiting for the army to arrive. The only thing going through her mind was her children's well-being. She vowed a terrible revenge upon Stormy if she hurt even a single hair on the twins' heads. *Oh, Alison. Why did you have to turn into Stormy? I want my sister back,* Angel thought with a tear in her eye. *I wish we never came to this time.*

Angel reminded herself this time is her time now. She couldn't change that. It didn't help her thoughts. She may well have to destroy her sister in order to get her children back. That turned her stomach. Well, she still had time to think on their trek to Natural Bridge Caverns. *No, it was now Nemesis,* she thought. And, the resulting interval scared her even more. They had only fifteen days to travel the nearly three hundred miles to Nemesis. *A distance that normally took at least sixteen days on foot,* she reflected. *Will we be in time?*

CHAPTER 6

Nemesis

THIRTEEN UNEVENTFUL DAYS PASSED SINCE they left the shack. It snowed twice in that time, but not enough to slow them down. Angel feared seeing the snow turning into ice. It hadn't happened and they were nearing their destination. Even so, anxiety threatened to overwhelm her. It was January 27. Three days remained for them to find the caverns. Time was not on their side, though they made better time than she imagined they would.

She called a temporary halt. "Cornellius, show me again where we are."

Barak handed him the map. Cornellius, being the most experienced with the area, pointed out their location. Angel nodded. Barak replaced the map in his pack and they started marching again. Hopefully they would get to the caverns before harm came to the twins.

That evening after their meal, Angel's mind kept turning to her children. She brooded over the time she felt they were wasting. To pass the time and keep herself from a panic, she sent a mental command to Seth. As she waited for him to appear, Niedra strode up and they walked over to the tent she shared with her husband. Angel sat on a nearby log while Niedra lounged next to her feet.

Seth approached the two and stretched out, lying face down in submission. Angel knew the respect he paid to both her and Niedra.

Are you still wanting to be Barak's friend? She asked him.

Yes, Angel.

She had to smile at that. Niedra was a good influence for her siblings. She stood and motioned Niedra to stay put. *Follow me, Seth.*

Barak and Avery sat near the main campfire conversing with Major Dag Ironstone, Barak's stonemason. Talk ceased when Barak caught sight of Angel walking up with Seth following.

"Barak, I have some unusual information to tell you."

His eyebrows rose as his glance went from the cat to Angel's face. At his nod, she continued.

"This is Seth. As you know, he is one of Niedra's siblings. What is so unusual is he has informed me he can hear your thoughts, Barak."

He stood and frowned. "What?"

Seth sat back and lowered his head in submission. Angel sensed this and smiled.

"Be at ease, my dwarf friend. As you can see, Seth is signaling his compliance to you. Before dismissing him, why don't you see if you can hear his thoughts?"

"But, what use have I with a cat?"

"Companionship?" Avery interjected, a smile on his face.

Barak glared a moment at Avery before turning back to Angel and Seth. Angel raised her eyebrows in question. She knew the turmoil roiling in Barak's mind without having to invade his thoughts. He snorted, surrendering to the inevitable.

"Very well," he rasped.

He appeared to be in a trance that lasted a few minutes. Suddenly, he laughed. Aloud he said, "Thank you, Seth. I accept."

"This is new," Avery said. "I wonder if the other cats can hear certain persons."

"We can experiment and see," said Angel.

"I never would have believed I'd be in contact with one of these dratted cats," Barak said roughly to hide his embarrassment. "Especially thinking of my past experiences with them," he added under his breath.

"We can ask Kalika if she knows anything about their past the next time we see her," Angel suggested. "We know they arrived with the Ancient Ones. Perhaps they've always had this ability. But, we proved dangerous to them. Consequently, they turned dangerous to us."

"That's a plan." Avery stood and moved toward Angel. "I think we should call this day over and get what sleep we can."

"Agreed." Barak bade them a good night before turning toward Seth, looking up at him but still at his feet.

Avery led Angel to their own tent. Niedra looked up as they entered and mewed quietly at them.

"Goodnight to you, too," Avery said.

Angel curled up next to her husband and knew she'd get very little sleep. Her mind stayed on her missing children and she quietly wept for them, her arms aching to hold them.

———

Four days later, Angel's anxiety turned to panic. It was the morning of the thirty-first, one day passed their deadline, and they still hadn't found the caverns. Avery tried to console her. She felt the panic and worry in him, too, and took comfort in his ability to control his emotions and not allow them to control him. She realized the only thing to do was trudge on.

An hour later, a man appeared in the middle of the road ahead of them. The cats surrounded him and he raised his hands in surrender. Mentally Angel spoke to the cats and, obeying her, they sat back, allowing the man to advance.

"Please don't harm me. I'm looking for an elf named Angel in the company of dwarves. Can you help me?"

Angel stepped forward. "I am she. What do you want?"

Barak stepped in front of her. "Don't think you can harm her, mister. All of us have pledged our lives to keep her safe." He swung his ax around and included the entire company in his gesture.

"I have no weapons, good sir. I was told to lead you to Nemesis."

"And what do you know of Nemesis?" Serylda asked. She joined her brother in front of Angel and held her quarterstaff at the ready.

The man shrugged. "It's a cave near here. I was told that was the name."

Angel placed a hand on each dwarf's shoulder and stepped in front of them. She turned toward the man. "How far is this cave?"

He beamed at her. "Not far. Only about ten miles."

"Are you hungry?" she asked him with a smile, sensing his condition.

"Oh, yes, ma'am! I ain't eaten in two days."

She turned to Barak. "Does this place look good enough for a rest stop?"

He nodded.

Angel turned to one of the dwarfs. "Take him to some water and food, please."

The man beamed at her and thanked her profusely as someone led him away for the promised meal. Serylda and Cornellius offered to accompany the stranger. The others settled for a brief rest while the man ate. In the meantime, Angel motioned for Avery and Barak to follow her off to one side.

"Well, I feel a lot better," she said. "He's a simpleton. I believe Stormy wanted to make sure we came."

"By sending a simpleton." Barak stated, always the skeptic.

"Yes," Avery said suddenly. "He'd be easier to control. He probably doesn't realize how evil she is. He'd do anything to please her."

Angel agreed. "If Stormy took the time to send someone to fetch us, maybe she hasn't done anything to the kids yet."

Cornellius strode up and joined them. "You want to hear something sad? He thinks she's a sweet little old lady that has a wonderful surprise for him if he can get you to Nemesis before the end of tomorrow at the latest."

"She'll probably kill him in some sick way," Barak rasped. "That'll be his *wonderful* surprise."

"I will not let that happen," Angel vowed. "He will be put in the medic squad for safety once we get there."

"He'll put up a fight," Cornellius interjected. "He wants his surprise."

"Let him," Barak said, agreeing with Angel. "I have the perfect man to guard him without realizing he's being guarded. Major Dag Ironstone."

Cornellius nodded. "Yes, he's the perfect man, alright. I have another idea that may help. Put them with Nicholas and Rick. They may be able to get more pertinent information out of the man." He laughed quietly. "Who knows? Ariel may be of some help, too."

"We'll do that when we reach Nemesis," Avery added. "Though he is childlike, we don't want our 'guide' to become suspicious before we reach the caverns."

Barak nodded and strode off. The others went back and joined the stranger still eating in the company of Serylda.

Angel squatted in front of the man and smiled. "What's your name?"

With a mouth full of food, he tried to smile back. "Norris Waller. But you can call me Nory."

"Alright, Nory." She rose to her feet. "Well, when you finish eating, we'll be on our way. Okay?"

"Okay. Thanks for the food." He placed the last morsel of food in his mouth and rose, rubbing his hands together. Swallowing, he added, "I'm ready. I can't wait to get you there. She said she had a surprise for me if I hurried. You see, I didn't get my Christmas present this year."

Angel let the man ramble on as everyone rose. The trek to Nemesis once more got underway as Nory led the dwarf army of seventy along with their leaders.

Nemesis. Angel thought on that name. Stormy had been a fan of the mythological stories their mother used to tell them when they were young. Was she giving Angel a message? Nemesis was the goddess of vengeance. Why else would she pick that particular name? And she believed Stormy would kill Nory. That would be his surprise. Angel just hoped her children were being treated decently. She dare not let herself think otherwise. Stormy had better treat the twins with respect. If they were harmed in any way, she didn't know what she would do to Stormy. She felt she may lose her sanity if she dwelled too much on the idea.

Nory proved to be an adequate guide. Around dusk on February 1, they arrived at their destination. About a mile from the cave, a company of two hundred of Stormy's men met them.

"That's far enough," one of them yelled and stepped forward.

"Who are you?" Barak yelled back. He unsheathed his ax. The rest of the dwarf army followed suit. Avery and Angel stood behind him while all six badgercats remained motionless behind them.

"A sentry. That is all you need to know, dwarf." He spat the word 'dwarf' like an obscenity, though he seemed to be uneasy at the sight of the cats. "I was told to lead a select few of you to Her Honor. The rest must remain here."

Angel noticed Stormy's men outnumbered them nearly three to one. *Not really bad if you consider what good fighters dwarves were,* she thought. *And in addition, we have six badgercats at our disposal.* She placed a hand on Barak's shoulder and moved to stand beside him.

"Who are the ones you seek?" she asked.

As Angel distracted Stormy's man, Barak whispered something to the major. Then he glanced over at Angel and barely nodded. She didn't have to read his thoughts to know what he was thinking. Major Ironstone would make Barak a great general someday. With his skills as a diplomat, the dwarves had someone special. The major led Nory into the midst of the army without a fuss.

"They are Angel, Avery, Barak, Cornellius, and Serylda. Oh, and a man named Norris Waller. He was supposed to find you and lead you here. She also said if you try to fool her she'd kill the brats."

Angel looked around, then back at the man. "I'm sorry but we don't know of a Norris Waller. The others you named are right here." She noticed the man had named the top people in the entourage. He left out the major, perhaps because Stormy didn't have knowledge of him. The five named persons stepped forward shifting the sentry's attention to them and away from Nory being led into the midst of the army.

"Lead on," Barak rasped. He stood in front of the man daring him to provoke a fight.

"Not yet, dwarf." He pointed at the ground. "You will leave your weapons here." He sneered. "Or the kids are dead."

"Do you promise to take us to Stormy safely?" Angel asked quickly. She placed a hand on Barak's arm and didn't need her power to sense Barak's feelings. She felt his desire for battle through her fingers.

The man scoffed. "That's why we're here."

"You can't trust them," Barak argued, unable to keep quiet.

"You have to, dwarf. Or you die here and the kids die, too," he taunted. "Oh, I almost forgot. If we don't make it inside Nemesis before sundown, the kids are dead. So, you'd better hurry and decide what you will do."

Subtly Angel used her power to touch the man's mind. He was telling the truth. Stormy had no compunction about killing the children in a little over an hour from now. Breaking contact with the man, she turned and nodded at Avery.

"We agree," Avery replied. He laid his weapon on the ground first. Angel placed her quarterstaff next to his weapon.

Angel looked Barak in the eye and pleaded silently. Grudgingly he nodded his agreement and placed his ax on the other side of Avery's bow. Serylda and Cornellius followed their example. The five straightened and glared at the man.

"Wait," the man said, delaying their departure. "There's still the problem of Norris Waller."

"Angel already told you no such man met us," Barak lied.

Angel shrugged at the guard.

"Well, who was that man you had escorted away?"

"Just someone from my country," Cornellius interjected. "He knew this terrain better than anyone else we knew. He led us here."

"Yes," Barak added. "I didn't want to be responsible for him coming to harm. His wife just had a baby and I want to see him home safely." He glared at the sentry, daring him to question the lie.

"Let's go!" the man yelled after a moment.

He led the way as Angel gave a quick order to the cats to stay put. The five followed close behind with the rest of Stormy's men bringing up the rear. They had an hour to get to the entrance of Nemesis and their meeting with Stormy.

With five minutes to spare, they were positioned just inside the cave entrance. Stormy herself stood in front of them and smirked. She dismissed her troops and the sentry led his men away to stand guard outside.

"Well, I see you finally made it." She turned and laughed. "I knew I could count on you, sis. Come. I have refreshments waiting."

CHAPTER 7

Confrontation

"**H**OW ARE MY CHILDREN?" ANGEL asked, unable to wait for Stormy to mention them first. She walked beside Stormy. The others fell in behind the two women.

Stormy snickered as she led them deeper into the cave. "Oh, don't worry, sis. I just wrote some date on that note. I knew you wouldn't let me down. Anyhow, I had a few of my sentries watch for your approach and to lead you here once they spotted you. I hope my Nory led you okay."

"He did fine."

"Yes, well," Stormy mused. "He was supposed to join you in coming inside. I guess I have some disciplining to do." She sighed. "Oh, well. Sometimes keeping everyone in line can be taxing."

"I put him into protective custody with my army," Barak barked.

"I already figured that out, dwarf," Stormy barked back. "But, still," she continued casually, "I did tell my guard that no matter what, Nory was to accompany you." She shrugged and snorted. "I blame him more than you, dwarf."

In silence she led them into a small room. Inside she had tables and chairs set up. At one end, Angel noticed what could only be called a throne. Slaves had placed goblets of drink and platters of food on the tables. Stormy grabbed a plate and dug in, piling on food to overflowing, then picking up a filled goblet went directly to the throne and sat, straddling her chair in an unladylike fashion. She motioned the others to serve themselves.

No one moved.

She raised her goblet in a toast and drank greedily from it. Some of the liquid dribbled down her chin. With the back of one hand, she wiped the juice off and sat the goblet down on the floor next to her chair. She shook her head and grunted once.

"Come on, everyone. I haven't poisoned the food or drink. I am trying to be civil. You'd better enjoy it. I rarely feel like company." She picked up a piece of meat from her plate and started to bite into it only to stop. "Oh, I almost forgot." She replaced the meat onto her plate and clapped her hands once. A minion led the twins into the room. They sat down at the table closest to Stormy and waited. The minion went to the food tables and filled two plates. He brought the plates and two goblets to the children and stood behind them after serving them.

"Hi, mom," Jared intoned as he began to eat.

"Hi," Janna copied her brother.

Angel dared not speak. She felt her sanity hanging by a thread. Fifteen years ago, she saw a malevolent aura surrounding her sister and Avery. This time it surrounded the twins. Her children were being manipulated by the evil that was in her sister. She needed to be strong for them.

"As you can see, they are perfectly fine. I've rather enjoyed their company." She placed her plate on the floor next to her goblet. Rising, she ambled over to stand next to the minion, waving him back toward the entry they had arrived from. "You should bring them to visit me more often, my dear sister." She placed a hand on each child's shoulder. "Such well-behaved children."

Angel repressed a shudder when Stormy touched her children. She perceived the evil aura grow around the twins and her hatred for her sister grew.

"Why did you keep us away from our aunt?" Janna was asking. "She's very nice to us."

"You were being very nasty by not allowing us to get to know our aunt," Jared added. "In fact, mother, she told us you want to kill her. Why?"

Angel didn't answer. Her heart was breaking.

Stormy scoffed and leered at her. "Children, perhaps your mom will answer that later. For now, since you're finished eating, why don't you go play?" She gave the twins each a pat on the shoulder before letting them go. She motioned the minion over and he led the children away.

Stormy's face grew hard. "Since no one wants to take advantage of my hospitality, you will be taken to a special place to contemplate your predicament." Snickering as she left, she signaled a guard to lead them to a different part of the caverns.

As each member of the company left the vicinity of Stormy, a guard appeared and trailed behind. All five prisoners ended up with a personal guard, the one charged to escort them led the assembly. The leader marched them deeper into the caves. The further they walked the darker it became, until only two torches remained ahead. The lead guard removed the nearest one, and holding it in front of him, led them even deeper through the gloomy halls. A door appeared out of the darkness. Taking a set of keys from a hidden pocket, the guard opened the door. Avery, Barak, and Cornellius were shoved inside and the guard locked them in the blackness.

The women were escorted ten paces further down the hall where another door appeared. Once more, the guard unlocked a door and shoved his prisoners inside. The women were left in the dark as they heard the door being locked and steps fading from their earshot.

"Now, what?" Serylda asked.

"I guess we wait."

Angel sensed the location of the dwarf and took hold of Serylda's hand. With outstretched hands Serylda led them to a wall and both women sat on the floor.

"I still have my ability to hear Avery."

"Good. We can stay in touch with the men," Serylda commented. "How are they faring?"

Avery?

I'm here. How are you two?

We are fine but are a little farther back into the caves. The guards left us in the dark like you.

Just stay calm. We can do no more than that.

I understand. Aloud Angel said, "The men are fine. Avery said to stay calm. Do you have a sense of time?"

"Yes. All dwarves do. You know that."

Time passed.

"How long has it been?" Angel asked, her voice loud in the silence.

"About ten hours. You fell asleep."

"Did you get any sleep yourself?"

"No. I may like caverns, but darkness isn't my favorite way to spend time in them."

"Nor mine, my friend."

Avery's voice broke into Angel's mind. *Someone is opening our door.* After a brief pause he added, *we have food.*

She heard the rattle of keys as their door was opened. The light from the torch burned their eyes. Angel moaned from the pain. Serylda scrambled toward the light just as the door was closed, shutting them back into darkness. Serylda scooted back to sit next to Angel, her hands held the tray left for them.

"We are not going to starve, it seems," Angel remarked. To Avery she sent a mental note that they had food, too.

Their tray held something that felt like crackers, something that smelled like cheese, and two goblets of water. Both girls finished the tray of food. They took turns relieving themselves in one corner. The dungeon room was becoming ripe with foul odors.

Again, time passed.

Having nothing to pass the time but sleep, they took turns. One stayed alert as the other napped.

When Angel awoke from her latest nap, she asked, "How long have we been in here now?"

"I believe one full day has passed."

They heard a noise outside the door. Keys rattled in the lock. A torch was thrust into the room. Both women squinted at the intrusion.

"Angel, you are to follow me to see Her Magnificence now."

She stood up and nodded. Following the sentry into the hall, she sent a quick note to Avery.

I think Stormy is ready to talk.

Be careful.

The light no longer hurt her eyes by the time they escorted her back into the small dining room. Stormy was seated atop her throne with a plate piled high. She gestured for Angel to help herself to a plate of food.

"I suggest you don't ignore my generosity this time."

Angel sighed. She walked up to the table and added some crackers and cheese to a plate. Taking a goblet, she half-filled it with the wine sitting at the end of the table. Taking her food to a table near Stormy, she sat, the food ignored.

"What do you want?" she asked Stormy.

"Just your company." Stormy took a big bite of some sort of meat. The juices dribbled down her chin. "I miss our time together, sister." She wiped the juice off with a napkin and gestured for Angel to eat.

"You know," Stormy continued, once Angel took a bite of cheese, "I'm not as bad as the Centauri makes me out to be. I offer you a chance to get to know the real me."

"You destroy things. How can you say you aren't evil?"

Stormy leaned forward, and with a harsh voice, said, "I have the same right to survive as everyone else does."

"At the expense of others?"

Stormy sat back and placed her plate on the floor, once more the gracious hostess. "If you let me inside your mind, I could let you see the real me."

"No." Angel ate one of her crackers. "I had a look into your mind when I defeated you with Ahriman."

"He was a fool. You saw mainly *his* mind, not mine." She drank deeply from her goblet and gestured for more. "Can you not see we are a lot alike?"

"How?"

Stormy laughed and grabbed the now-full goblet from the sentry, spilling some onto the floor. She took another deep drink before remarking, "Since I share your sister's mind, I know you, Angela. And, yes, I called you by your real name, not the one the Centauri gave you. Being inside your sister, I know your weaknesses, and your strengths. You cannot hide from me now."

Angel laughed. "Well, if you really know me, you would know you just threw down the proverbial gauntlet. I don't trust you, Zaxcellian. And as *you* can see, I know you as well."

Stormy leaned forward. "Are you sure you don't want to know the real me? I can make you powerful."

"I'm sure you think you could. But, no thank you. I will just enjoy your hospitality." Angel bit into a piece of cheese, and surprising herself calmly asked, "How are the kids?"

"They are well-behaved kids. I believe you and your elf husband did a good job of rearing them." Stormy took another sloppy bite of her meat, again letting the juice dribble down her chin. This time she left it there. "It's your loss, getting to know the real me."

Angel nibbled on a cracker.

Stormy sighed noisily. "Well, I'm disgusted with trying to get you to see reason. Alison said you'd be like this. But I thought I could change your mind." She gestured at one of her guards. "Take her back to her cell."

Angel rose and followed the guard with no more words exchanged between her and Stormy. Once back inside the black cell, she sat down beside Serylda.

"What did she want?" the dwarf asked.

"She tried to be civil. But, in reality, it was the Zaxcellian who tried to befriend me. Even told me the Centauri were making *them* out as evil."

"I hope you didn't fall for that."

"No." Angel chuckled. "In fact, she returned me here because I basically ignored her."

"Good for you." Angel felt the dwarf settle in for the time being. "We should probably get some rest."

"Yes," Angel replied. "Especially since there's nothing else to do."

Time passed.

Angel kept in touch with Avery. The men talked the time away, bored but fine. She let him know they were fine, also. Twice someone brought them food, the only occasion they saw any light.

— ᳇ᵕᵕᵕᵕᵕᵕᵕᵕᵕ —

Angel learned from Serylda they had been locked in the dungeon for nearly three days when they heard many footsteps. Several guards showed up. Opening their cell, the torches were over bright to their dark sensitive eyes. After leading them to men's cell, one guard ordered them to stand still while another opened it letting the men out to the bright torches. Squinting, Avery nodded at Angel to let her know they were fine. She returned the gesture.

The guards led them to the same small room Stormy had offered them food. She sat on the throne eating, as usual her plate full to overflowing. Again she motioned them to help themselves to something on the buffet. No one moved.

Stormy's face grew hard. "Fine. We shall have our little talk now." She practically threw her plate onto the floor, breaking the dish, and rose. One of her minions stooped to clean up the mess. "Let's get down to business. Follow me."

She led them to an adjacent room, one slightly larger than the previous room but also sporting a throne. Nothing else furnished the room. On her right, Angel spotted a doorway into another passage where the largest wolf she had ever seen came strolling out.

"Ah, yes." Stormy placed her right hand on the wolf's head. Changing from anger to cheerfulness she gestured at the animal. "Meet my pet. His name is Wolfy. Isn't he beautiful?" She laughed. "I know. The name isn't very original. But, what do you think of my new home, and the name I chose for it?" She drew in a deep breath and let it out loudly but slowly. "Nemesis. It fits nicely, I think." She laughed, spread her arms wide and made a circle, strolled to the throne and sprawled onto it. The animal followed her and took a place at her feet. "You do like the color scheme I chose, I hope."

"Not particularly," Angel answered for the group. She kept her voice soft and nonthreatening. "I recognize this ugly shade of red as the same one you used in Attor." She stood with the others near the entrance.

"It's ghastly," Serylda commented. "It's like you painted the room in blood."

Stormy laughed and leaned forward. "I really don't care what you think, dwarf. And that is the reason I did away with that elfin scum you were betrothed to." She sighed, leaned back and crossed her legs. "I think that was some of my best work. Don't you think so, my dear sister?"

Serylda snarled and took a step toward the throne. Angel shook her head and placed a hand on Serylda's shoulder. She felt the rage Serylda kept barely in check. At the same time, the wolf bared his teeth and growled. Barak took Angel's place beside his sister, placing a hand on her arm. Avery stood on Serylda's other side ready to offer help, if needed, to control her. Angel stepped forward until she stood only a few feet away from Stormy and the wolf.

"You said you wanted to get down to business. What do you want?" Angel sensed the patience in her friends breaking down. *Time to confront the Zaxcellian*, she thought, *before it gets ugly in here.*

Stormy shrugged. "Nothing much really. Just your obedience and their deaths."

"What will their deaths accomplish?"

"Oh, I don't know. Maybe it's because I've always been jealous of you."

Angel frowned. "In what way?" She knew she wasn't talking to her sister. Instead, it was the Centauri enemy, the Zaxcellian, in control of

Alison. *Perhaps the Zaxcellian's control was weakening*, she thought. *It's talking to me as if it was Alison. I can only hope that perhaps our talk the other day has caused a reaction in the alien.*

Stormy studied Angel a moment. "You've always been able to make friends. I haven't. I've always hated you for that."

"Alison..." Angel began. The alien sounded unsure of itself.

Stormy rose. "My name is Stormy!" she raged. Just as suddenly, she calmed down and reseated herself. "Don't ever forget that."

Angel used the alien's uncertainty on it. "I'm sorry. I'll always think of you as my sister, Alison. I can't help it. If, as you said, you know me because of Alison, you'd know I speak truly."

"Well, just don't call me that and we'll get along fine." Stormy's eyes grew to slits. Angling her head sideways, she added, "Yes, I think we could get along reasonably if you would listen to me for a change. I am in charge. My men listen to me. Your children listen to me." Stormy nodded. "You will, too."

"Why do you think I'll listen to you?" Angel sensed the Zaxcellian was definitely losing control. It began repeating itself. Angel used that to her advantage.

Stormy chortled. "You just will. Since I have control of your brats, I can kill them easily. Just as easily as I plan to kill your friends. Then you will have no one to rely on except me." She recrossed her legs and leered. "You see? I'm the one in control."

A thought entered Angel's mind. Was the Zaxcellian losing itself being inside a human? It thinks it is Alison, her sister. Was that the reason for its irrational behavior? *It is centuries old*, she reminded herself.

"How do you propose to control me, sister?"

Stormy laughed. "The same way I control your brats and my men."

"You said that already. May I remind you, you tried to control me when you were Ahriman? It didn't work then. It won't work now."

"I hate to say it, but you're right. Nonetheless, as your sister, I know you. Also, I have leverage now I didn't have then. You forget your friends and kids."

"No, I haven't forgotten them."

Uncrossing her legs, Stormy leaned forward until she was inches from Angel's face. "Maybe I need to do something about your friends now. Then you'll know I'm serious. I'm so going to enjoy killing them. And, you, my dear, are going to watch."

"No!" Serylda raged, unable to restrain herself. Avery and Barak barely had the strength to contain her.

Stormy rose, suddenly in a rage herself, and pointed. "You can be first, dwarf. I've waited a long time for this." She lunged toward Serylda only to run into Angel. They went down in a jumble of arms and legs. The wolf growled and bared his teeth in their faces.

At the moment of contact, Angel sensed the duality in her sister's body. The evil thing known as Stormy was the Zaxcellian Kalika warned her of, the evil entity she remembered when she confronted Ahriman fifteen years ago. It vacated Alison and entered Angel's mind. Caught off guard by the sudden attack, Angel let go of Alison. She left her lying on the floor and rose to her hands and knees. A violent struggle developed inside her mind. The Zaxcellian proved strong. Angel made a desperate plea toward Kalika in the caverns so far away. The Centauri sent a piece of herself to join Angel's body and the struggle for control ensued.

Two things saved Angel, her knowledge of the Zaxcellian's need to destroy all humans and the strength to repel the Zaxcellian. Both came from the part of the Centauri she now harbored. Looking up into the face of the wolf, it stared back in confusion. A moment later, the beast bared its teeth and lunged at her. With the help of Kalika, Angel gained control for a split second and grabbed the animal's head inches from her own. She pushed the evil Zaxcellian into the beast as it tried to fight back. The wolf howled and backed away. Angel slumped next to her sister. Placing a hand on Alison's brow, she blocked out the evil Zaxcellian from them both not realizing Kalika had locked it inside the wolf, leaving Angel and Alison free of the vile entity. The wolf howled again and backed farther away.

It made the mistake of backing into Serylda's legs. Going berserk, she broke free of the hold the males had on her and withdrew a hidden knife. With blind fury she plunged the knife deep into the wolf. All her pent-up hatred she had carried through the years fueled her rage as she stabbed the animal over and over even as it mauled her. Moments later, the battle was over. With the wolf dead and herself still in a berserker rage, Serylda looked around and spotted Angel comforting a weeping Alison.

Serylda growled and bared her teeth. "Get away from her." But, before she could react, she collapsed to her knees from the loss of blood.

Angel looked at her. "It's over, Serylda," she said quietly. "Don't you see? Don't you understand? It was Stormy we were to destroy, not Alison. Your enemy, our enemy, is dead beneath your knife. Stormy is gone. You fulfilled your oath by killing the Zaxcellian, the true evil. The fighting is over."

Serylda dropped her knife as the rage left her eyes and Angel's quiet words sank into her consciousness. The others rushed to her side and hastily bandaged her many wounds. Angel watched while comforting her sister. When they finished bandaging Serylda, Angel rose and helped Alison to her feet. Cornellius aided Serylda weak from her loss of blood and the berserker rage that had consumed her earlier. He helped her onto the throne where she collapsed.

"Let's go find the children," Angel said anxiously. "I need them near me."

I'm going after my army, in case we need them," Barak said, and left. Cornellius and Serylda followed him at a slower pace.

Avery, Angel, and Alison went in search of the children. Alison couldn't recall where they were, the evil Zaxcellian kept the Alison soul from knowing many things. They found two of Stormy's listless and wandering men, and forced them to lead them to the children. Along the way, Avery informed the men that Stormy was destroyed by the Alastrine Savior. They stole a glance at Alison and knew the words were true.

"I guarantee your safety if you never take up arms again in your lifetime," Avery promised the men. "Just take us to the children."

They found the frightened twins, no longer in the alien's control, and placed them in their parents' custody. Once done, they made their way out of the caverns.

Angel looked back at the entrance to the caverns. She felt thankful for some reason that these caverns still retained their ancient visage. The Zaxcellian didn't destroy them as it did Yellowstone.

Cornellius and the group of badgercats greeted them. The twins were ecstatic to see their pet and amazed to see the strange cats in Jamala's company. It didn't stop the children from greeting the wild animals just as enthusiastically as they did Jamala.

They learned they had been inside the caverns four days. Angel looked up at the clear night sky. The stars twinkled brightly. Her children were safe and she had her sister back. Alison had permission to share Serylda's tent. That surprised Angel. Cautiously, Angel touched the dwarf's mind and smiled. Her sister was in good hands. *You're in good hands, too, my dwarf friend,* she thought. Both needed healing.

CHAPTER 8

The Twins' Story

THAT EVENING THEY SAT BY a roaring fire, no longer in need to be careful. Cornellius and his two falcons left on a hunt. They came back with enough rabbits to feed everyone. The food rotated on spits as a pot sat boiling with potatoes and other root vegetables. They waited for the meal to be ready and chatted about the latest events. Angel wanted to hear the twins' story of why they didn't wait at Damek.

"You have some explaining to do," Angel began. "I want to know why you didn't obey us this time."

"Wait, Angel," Avery interrupted. "Let's move somewhere more private."

"Agreed." Angel saw his need to keep their problems with the children as private as possible. No one else really needed to know the particulars of the twins' misbehavior. Barak nodded his understanding as the four left the fire.

They found a log nearby but far enough away to guarantee no one could eavesdrop on their conversation. Avery maneuvered the twins onto a log across from Angel and himself. Janna stared at the ground, not saying anything. Jared just regarded their mother. Angel didn't need to use her powers to sense their shame of their disobedience.

"Come on. It's not going to get any easier. Just start telling us what happened," Angel prodded.

"We were missing both you and dad," Jared said simply, and shrugged.

"And decided we could follow your trail with Jamala's help," Janna added, quietly. "We didn't mean to get into trouble. I convinced Jared we could find you."

"Yeah, two days after you left, we had decided to go after you," Jared began. "Sneaking out was the easy part."

———————

"Come on, Janna," Jared whispered, nearly running into her. "This was your idea, remember? Don't stop now. We're almost clear. We need to get out of this swamp before it gets too dangerous." He pulled on the horse's reins and followed Janna.

"Stop badgering me," Janna whispered back harshly while sidestepping a root.

Jared urged the horse on. He kept his eyes on Jamala, their pet badgercat, now several feet ahead. It wouldn't do to lose her now. She led them past the alligator dens and quicksand pits that surrounded Damek's swamps with ease.

Janna shuddered. "I sure wish I had eyes like Jamala. I hate the dark, especially since there's no moonlight to see by. I just don't see how she does it."

Jared shrugged. "She's an animal. What did you expect? Just keep up with her, okay? Don't lose her in here. It's too dark for us to find our way out of here if you do." He reached back and patted the now skittish horse. "You do realize how much trouble we'll be in when we get there, don't you?"

"I don't care, and I know you don't either. If you did, we'd be back in our room and not out here." She climbed over a low lying branch. "I miss mom and dad and so do you. And, don't worry, I won't lose Jamala. I'm smarter than that. Besides, if we lose her, she'd just come find us. Though we can't talk to her, she hears us like Niedra hears mom."

With a little help from Janna, Jared persuaded the horse to climb over the same branch. He scrambled over and took the reins back. "Look," he said in a normal voice. "We've made it out and without the moon's help."

She stuck her tongue out at his smile. He laughed. A few moments later, she joined in the laughter. She couldn't stay mad at her twin. She reached over and patted their cat, saying, "Good girl." Since Jared had spoken in a normal voice, she did too. Facing him once more, she sighed. "I sure hope Jamala can lead us to mom and dad. I guess it doesn't matter which way. She'll find the trail." Janna put her head near the cat's big head and thought to the animal, *Find Niedra.*

The cat mewed quietly and trotted off. "I guess we go west," Jared said and shrugged. They mounted the now calm horse and followed closely behind their pet.

The twins traveled through the night and into the next evening. They relied on the sure-footed horse since the moon set shortly after dusk. Janna remarked, not for the last time, how she hated the dark, but like her brother, was anxious to find their parents.

"In another two weeks, we'll enjoy a full moon," Jared remarked.

"Well, I hope we find mom and dad before then," Janna said.

They stopped twice and ate some dried meat and drank some of the juice they swiped from Nicholas's kitchen. They promised each other they'd pay him back for their pilfering the next time they saw him.

The children began day four tired and hungry. They had been living on what berries they found for the last two days and ate the last of the dried meat the night before. It was November 13 and they'd be lucky to find anything else to satisfy their hunger.

"How much farther do we have to go?" Janna whined.

"I told you I don't know. I figured we'd be there by now."

"Well, can't you find us something to eat?"

"I wish I could. I'm hungry, too, Janna. I don't know what to do. So, just stop complaining, will you?"

Janna sniffed once. "I want mom."

Jared threw up his hands in disgust. "Do you want to turn back?"

"No," she whispered.

"Then, please, don't start your crying." Jared stared at his sister a moment before he took her in his arms and comforted her. "I know how you feel. But we need to be brave and act like adults. Gee, we're almost twelve. Let's show everyone we're old enough to take care of ourselves."

Janna sniffed and straightened up. "I'm sorry. You're right. I'm willing to go a little farther tonight and then rest."

"Agreed." Jared smiled and gave her one more hug before letting her go. He urged the horse into a fast walk. Jamala mewed and led the way.

Janna looked up. The clouds hid what moonlight they had. "Do you think it'll rain?"

Jared looked up then, too. "I sure hope not. We'll try to find some kind of shelter just in case."

"Maybe Jamala can find us something?" Janna suggested.

They had no success in finding any decent shelter and slept under a sky full of ominous clouds. Their luck held that night. For the next day, they awoke cold but dry.

Two days later, they crossed the Crimson Marsh. Replenishing their water skins, they made their way through the swamp and on toward Jasper. They had no luck in finding much to eat and trudged on. Each day, Jared found a brush with a handful of fruit to fill the empty holes in their stomachs while Jamala led them to water. Luckily, the fruit wasn't poisonous. But at the pace they traveled, they feared they'd starve before finding their parents.

Around noon on November 20, they came across a small campfire. Dismounting, they hoped they'd find something, anything to fill their empty stomachs. Relying on the few berries and scarce water supplies along the trail was proving to be not enough. Jared tied the horse to a nearby tree while Jamala wandered around in the brush.

Jared inhaled sharply. "This is a battlefield."

"And how do you know that?" Janna stood with her hands on her hips. "I see no bodies. Just that campfire over there."

"Use your nose, sister." Both sniffed deeply. "Do you smell that? It's the stink of death. I remember that smell from a dead rabbit I found once."

Janna snorted. "How could you remember that? We were only three when that happened. I was there and I don't remember this smell then."

Jared rolled his eyes. "Why do you always have to question everything I say?"

She crossed her arms. "I guess you could be right." She wrinkled her nose and walked over to the horse and remounted. "Now that I think about it, that stench smells dirty, like a disease or something. Ugh!"

Glaring at his sister a moment, he shook his head and mounted behind her. He whistled for Jamala and, once more, urged the horse to follow the cat. They traveled for an hour longer before making camp. The cat went off to hunt while Jared gathered sticks for a fire needed this night. The sky spitted snow at them and they were once again unsuccessful at finding adequate shelter.

"When will you give up trying to do that?" Janna stood near the horse and watched Jared struggle with starting a fire. The contented animal nibbled dead grass near the tree Jared tied it to. Annoyed with her twin, Janna turned and took two blankets off the saddle and dusted off a nearby log. She wrapped herself in one of the blankets and sat down, holding the other blanket on her lap. "Why didn't you listen better to Nicholas when he was trying to teach you how to do that?"

Jared ignored her. He made a sizeable pile of the twigs and leaves. Looking around, he chose two rocks that looked about right. Rubbing the rocks together, he tried producing sparks with no success.

Janna snickered. "You can't even make the rocks spark. Are you sure you have the right kind?" She closed her eyes and snuggled deeper into her blanket.

Jared stood. "Can't you stop complaining and help? Oh, I forgot, you didn't want to learn how to make a fire."

She glanced up long enough to stick her tongue at him before retreating back into her blanket. From the blanket Jared heard," I don't need to learn. I'm a female."

"When did that matter? Mom can build a fire better than Dad." He leaned closer to her bundled form. "And she's female." He turned back to his task. Moments later he threw the rocks as hard as he could. Disgusted, he joined Janna on the log with his face cupped in his hands.

She handed him the other blanket, saying, "We should've stayed in Damek."

"Kind of late now, don't you think?" he retorted, taking the blanket.

She shivered and hugged herself. "I'm hungry. I'm thirsty. I'm tired. And, I'm freezing. I wish we had spent more time trying to find some kind of shelter for the night."

"Me, too." No longer in an argumentative mood, Jared, now nestled inside his blanket, pulled her down to the ground and snuggled up to her. They leaned up against the log. Shortly, Jamala returned from her hunt.

"At least one of us has eaten," Janna said quietly.

"Two, you mean." He pointed to the horse. Their jovial mood returning, they grinned at each other.

The cat settled down at their feet. Her warmth helped. Jared took both blankets and combined them. He tucked them around Janna and himself. Exhaustion and hunger overcame them and they quickly fell asleep.

The cat's sudden growl instantly brought them awake. They glanced up to see three crude-looking men staring at them, the unlit fire between themselves and the ruffians.

"Well, what have we here?" one man asked. "They look cold to me."

A second one knelt, being careful to keep the cold campfire between him and the twins. "We won't hurt you. Are you hungry? We have a camp a short walk from here. Would you care to join us?"

Janna jumped up, pulling both blankets with her. She threw one of them back at her brother. "Could we? We're starving. We haven't had much to eat in over a week."

Jared rose, tucking his blanket around his form, and grabbed Janna's arm. The cat gave a quiet growl at his sudden move. "Wait, Janna." He turned to the men. "How do we know we can trust you? And what happened to our horse?"

Janna gasped and searched the area. Jared was right. The horse was gone!

The man shrugged and rose. "I don't know anything about a horse. Maybe you didn't tie it up well enough and it wandered off. Anyway, your cat seems at ease with us."

"Aren't you afraid of her?" Jared asked. "She is a badgercat, you know."

"Yeah, we can see that," said the first man. "We can also see you two are elves. We've heard stories about elves befriending badgercats. It looks like the stories are true."

The second man leered and showed a mouthful of rotten teeth. "Well, how about it? We will trust you not to turn your animal on us. So, trust us. Besides, looks like you two need help if your horse ran off."

Janna turned to Jared. "I'm hungry and they did say they'd feed us." She pulled away from her brother, far enough for his hand to fall away. "And, anyway, we do have Jamala to protect us. Just like that man said." She pointed to the second man.

"Well, okay," Jared said, still not convinced of their honesty. But, like Janna, he was too hungry to argue. He moved to stand beside his sister, adding, "I still don't trust you."

The second man nodded in agreement. "Of course, I understand. We all have to survive in our own way out here in the wild." He brushed past them and ignored the cat. "C'mon. It's this way. We'll lead so you can keep a watchful eye on us. Okay?"

"Fine." Jared took hold of Janna's hand and beckoned the man and his companions to proceed. He gestured for the cat to follow next and they trailed after the cat.

An hour later the twins relaxed with full bellies from the hearty stew the men shared with them. They even gave Jamala some meat. Jared thanked them for their hospitality and stood to leave with Janna.

The third man hadn't said anything until now. "You don't have to go. You will stay with us." He leered, showing less teeth in his mouth than the second man. "In fact, we insist you stay."

The twins turned back and stared at the men, fear mirrored in their eyes. All three men held knives. They never felt in danger until that moment.

"Jamala!" Jared exclaimed. Janna followed her twin's line of sight and saw the big cat lying on her side. She appeared very sick. The kids rushed to their pet's side, their fear of the knives overpowered by their concern for Jamala. The cat lay unconscious and barely breathing. They tried sending thoughts to the cat to no avail.

The third man snorted "You can forget that cat of yours. I poisoned it with that piece of meat. She's not going anywhere." He ordered the other two to bind the children's hands. They led the tearful twins north and abandoned Jamala where she lay.

───────※◦◦◎◦◦※───────

"They made us walk all night," Jared finished. "By that morning, we couldn't walk any farther, so they let us ride in front of them on their horses."

Janna shuddered. "I hope I never have to experience that again."

Jared nodded in agreement. "They stank really bad, like they had some kind of terrible disease."

"Anyway, we ended up in Amar a day before Nicholas showed up," Janna added. "I'm glad he did, too. That day I overheard the owner telling someone about making me work in bedrooms with his clients. I didn't like the sound of that." She shuddered again.

"They meant prostitution, didn't they?" Jared asked.

"I'm afraid so, kids." Avery took a deep breath and sighed it away. "You two were luckier than you realize. I hope this has taught you two a lesson. You are not yet adults. Also, as you found out the hard way, Jamala may be a badgercat but that doesn't guarantee she will be there for you. She isn't always the best defense. Concerning the missing horse, I'll let that be." Avery rose.

"C'mon. Enough lecturing for now. Let's go eat. Cornellius is signaling to us that dinner is ready."

They headed for the promised food. After they ate and cleaned up, Avery walked them to their tent. He beckoned the twins inside.

"Get into your sleeping bags and go to sleep. I want to leave before first light. Your mother and I will be inside shortly."

Both children bade their parents 'goodnight' before obeying their father. Angel sighed as they walked some distance away from the tent to talk quietly out of the children's earshot.

"What do you think?" she asked.

Avery shook his head. "They're headstrong. Perhaps that is a good thing."

"Do you not feel any anger at their disobedience to us?"

"Well, a little, yes." He grunted once, then laughed quietly. "I can't stay mad at them. Can you?"

"No. But they need some kind of punishment, I think." She frowned and shook her head. "Perhaps they learned a good lesson. One well enough they won't do such a foolish thing ever again."

Avery pulled her close. "You are as soft as I."

She smiled at her husband. "We're some team, huh?"

"Yeah," he said, and quietly kissed her before letting her go. "Ready for sleep?"

"I'll come to bed in a moment."

She watched as Avery entered the tent. She sat down on a nearby log. She was blessed to have such a family. Today had been a busy one. Her children were safe with their father. She had her sister back after years of Alison being possessed by the terrible Zaxcellian. Her sister and her best friend now slept in the same tent though each had promised to kill the other. Luck seemed to be shining on them for a change.

Angel sighed, rose from the log she sat upon, and joined her family. Just before entering the tent, she looked back up at the sky and said a quick prayer of thanks. She would worry about the rest of their unfinished business in the morning. It had turned out to be an unexpected day. Were they finally rid of the danger they had faced for so many years? *Only time will tell*, Angel thought as she fell asleep in her husband's arms, her children safely snuggled nearby.

CHAPTER 9

More Decisions

T HE NEXT MORNING ANGEL WOKE to find Avery missing from their
bed. Her children slept soundly beside her. Quietly, so as not to
wake them, she crept out of the tent. A crisp clear morning greeted
her. The sky grew lighter as she gazed at the moon and drew in a deep
breath. The moon shone in her last quarter raiment and the winter
birds welcomed her with their songs. The day promised warmth
despite it being February 5.

Someone had already stoked the fire and it looked inviting. She
smelled the coffee coming from the steaming pot off to one side of the
fire. She stretched and ambled over to the group surrounding the fire
pit. Avery met her and gave her his cup. She thanked him and took a seat
next to her sister. He retrieved another cup and filled it before joining
her on the log.

Alison looks better this morning. Almost her old self, Angel thought.
She had given up hope of ever getting Alison back. *But even in this time,*
Angel had to remind herself, *nothing was impossible.* They were all well
on their way to accepting Alison in their midst. She only had to watch
Serylda for a little longer. Last night, Angel probed the dwarf's mind,
something she shied away from. She had to know Serylda's true feelings
concerning Alison before allowing them to share the same tent. In
killing the wolf, Serylda dispelled most of the dwarf vengeance she held
onto for the past fifteen years. But, she didn't trust Alison yet.

Probably never will after Alison, as Stormy, killed Javas, Angel
thought. Even so, she felt acceptance slowly growing inside her friend.

Sitting across from her, Barak nodded. "Good morning.
Beautiful day."

"Yes, it is," Angel agreed. "It'll be even better when this whole affair
is over."

"Yes, the sooner, the better," Serylda added and finished her coffee. She put her mug down and asked, "What's our plan for today?"

"It's up to Angel," Barak answered.

"Not you, Barak?" Angel retorted.

He smirked at her in answer.

So they're depending on me once again, she thought. *And, they're all staring at me.* She tried to gauge each person's feelings without probing. She skipped Avery knowing his thoughts. He'd support her as before. Seated on the other side of Avery, Serylda had been willing to kill for her and still would. Barak, now Dwarflord of Jasper, was anxious for his kinsmen, the trapped Bomani clan, and their guests. She couldn't deny she felt the same. She had no idea how Cornellius felt as he absentmindedly rubbed the feathers of one of the two falcons he had temporarily accepted as his own, his thoughts on the birds. One was perched on his leg while the other perched in a tree above him. He took a sip of his coffee as Angel transferred her attention to Alison. Her sister sat staring into the coffee mug she held between her knees, her coffee growing cold.

Niedra came up between Angel and Avery and began purring. She reached up and petted the big cat's head. The cat's orange eyes bore into hers.

All okay? Niedra asked mentally.

I don't know, my pet.

Your sister is here now. Does that not make you happy? I like when you are happy.

I know.

Why are the others worried? The cat sat back on its haunches.

We still have things to work out, my faithful friend. Why don't you go join your siblings and find something to eat? I'll be fine.

Niedra mewed softly, rose and ambled away.

Angel turned to the group. "Alison, do you harbor any ideas of what Stormy had planned? Anything would help."

"I'm not sure what you mean," she said as she glanced at Angel, a frown on her face.

"Did Stormy have any biological or chemical weapons stored in Attor?"

Alison's frown grew. "I think I recall something biological. But," she shook her head, "I'm not really sure about it."

"Well, what about its hiding place?"

Alison thought harder, her eyes closed in concentration. Opening them, she sighed. "I'm sorry. I can't recall where it was. It seems the longer I'm myself, the more of Stormy I forget." She put her mug down, the coffee gone cold, and placed her face in her hands.

Angel gave her a reassuring pat on the back. "Don't worry about it. We'll solve the problem."

Serylda rose, and after retrieving Alison's mug, put it with her own next to the fire. "I still don't trust you, Alison." She resumed her seat and asked, "Are you sure there isn't something you're not telling us?"

For once Alison looked straight at Serylda. Her devil-may-care attitude showed a little. "I assure you, I don't remember much of Stormy's thoughts and plans now. Like I said already, I think there may have been some sort of biological weapon in Attor. What or where it is, I haven't a clue. I will do my best in helping to find it. This is my world now, too." She spread her hands wide. "And I don't want to see it hurt anymore, not now." She let her hands drop to her lap, once again sad. "Serylda, I can't take back what evil I did. But, since I was forced to remember every evil deed I participated in, I'll do my best to right the wrongs. And, maybe, just maybe, someday you'll be able to forgive me."

The dwarf exhaled loudly. "We'll see. In deference to your sister, I promise to be civil to you unless you do something to change my mind."

"That's more than I deserve." Alison bowed her head toward the dwarf. "Thank you."

"Okay," Angel once more captured everyone's attention. "There's one more thing that's got me worried. We need to find out what's happened at Boman. I know Barak is as worried about his kin as I am about mine."

Barak nodded. "I've been thinking on that. I'll send thirty five men to Boman with Major Dag in command. As everyone knows, he's my master builder besides being one of my best fighters. Almost as good as myself. He'll know what to do if there's any trouble. And he can send word back to us concerning the condition of the caves. That will leave us forty men to do our job."

"Okay," Avery said. "As it stands, we go first to Attor and check out this bomb. Then we head for Boman. Right?"

"It's a plan," Alison said, cautiously trying to be a part of the conversation.

"Yes," Angel agreed, patting her sister's hand. Everyone rose with her. "Let's get this camp up and moving." She took hold of Avery's arm as everyone dispersed. "I'd like to send the children and Ariel with the army. They can be dropped off at Damek. If I know Cornellius, he'll insist the army stop and get supplies there."

Avery nodded. "I'll go see Cornellius now."

Before he made one step in that direction, Barak strode up with Cornellius, Nicholas, and two dwarf soldiers in tow. "Angel, Avery, these men here have news concerning Boman. I thought it best we all hear it together."

"Sergeant?" Avery prompted.

"Sire, Madam." The man bowed. "Private Rockwell here has come from Krikor and Boman."

"Tell me," Angel demanded, apprehensive for some reason.

"Krikor has been razed to the ground," said Private Rockwell, the second soldier, his uniform dirty and torn. A bandage covered his left forearm. "Nothing remains."

"Have you heard anything about Boman helping out?" Barak asked.

"I come from Boman, sire," he said. He stole a quick look at Alison before continuing, "I was sent by Devlak to inform you of the happenings. It was I who brought Devlak and the Lunn brothers to see my dwarflord."

———— ∽∾⧫⊙⊙⧫∽∾ ————

On November 7, Devlak Blackstone, accompanied by Merwyn and Derwyn Lunn and their two badgercats left immediately from Damek for the Boman caverns on horseback. Even with the horses, it took nearly half a month for them to reach the caverns in the east. Upon arrival, they were brought before Dwarflord Boden Greyrock.

"Sire, I have dire news and a favor to ask of you," Devlak began with a bow. At Boden's nod, he continued. "Queen Angel bade me and her faithful servants, the Lunn brothers, to come here and ask for your help. We were told by one of Stormy's men that Krikor was to be destroyed."

"Yes, I had heard such a rumor myself. One of my men came across an army on the other side of the Ozarks." He gestured at the dwarf who had showed Devlak and company to Dwarflord Boden's presence. "Private Rockwell here overheard one of their sentries talking about destroying Krikor. He hurried back to tell me. I've been awaiting the call to war ever since. But I had expected it to happen sooner than this."

"We come straight from Falconland, sire," said Merwyn.

"We assumed our people would have sent you a messenger as they sent us word in Damek," said Derwyn.

Boden frowned. "No messenger arrived. However, I have had my army on standby, awaiting for someone to inform us, whether or not, we go to war."

The dwarflord rose and escorted the three men to some food. He sent the private to inform the army that they were marching to war. Anxious to begin, the Bomani dwarves gave a great shout, rattling the cavern walls. By the time the messengers had eaten their fill, the Bomani army had reached the surface, ready to march to Krikor. Devlak and the Lunn brothers joined the army and the march to Krikor began.

The enemy had pushed the Elfin Nation, fleeing from their beloved city, to within five days on foot from Boman before Devlak, the Lunn brothers, and the Bomani army led by their dwarflord found them on a rainy November 25. A little more than half the elves had survived the running battle, young and old perishing in the evacuation. The dwarf army worked their way through the refugees urging them on. In the process, Devlak learned the enemy was closer than he imagined and the elfin army was having a hard time keeping them at bay. Pressing on, he noticed that the sight of Dwarflord Boden and his doughty warriors in the company of the Lunn brothers gave the Elfin Nation the extra strength and courage to keep going despite the rain.

Upon reaching the elfin army, Devlak and Boden hunted for the captain.

"Tell me what happened," Devlak demanded. The Lunn brothers with their cats stood behind Devlak. Merwyn nodded and the captain gave his testimony.

The last of the elves rushed into the Keep as two others slammed the huge doors shut. Stormy's men had taken a toll on the Elfin Nation that day. One fourth of them would never again walk this earth. The enemy troops surrounded the Keep in moments. The siege of Krikor had begun.

Two elves escaped the Keep the next evening under the cover of rain clouds. One rode south, the other rode east. The elves on the battlements watched as Stormy's general sent troops to kill the scouts. It was to no avail. The horses on which the elves rode were Krikor's finest and fastest. Nothing on earth could catch them. Nothing that is, except arrows.

The southbound elf carried two stuck in his side for several miles. The elves on the wall prayed he would make it to Falconland before he died. The king and queen had to know what was happening to their kingdom.

The eastbound elf made it safely past Stormy's troops. It was up to him to rally help from Boman. He couldn't fail. If he couldn't persuade Dwarflord Greyrock to aid them, the Elfin Nation was doomed.

Meanwhile, back at the Keep, Stormy's men threw flaming balls of pitch over the walls that the rain failed to quench. The men working the trebuchet were never allowed to rest. When one collapsed from exhaustion another would take his place. They were going to burn the elves in their beloved city. The sun came out, however several days passed before the vegetation finally caught fire. The elves had kept the fires under control for as long as they could. In the end, the flaming balls proved too much.

After two weeks of battle, the time to flee had come to pass. It was to the elves good fortune that it happened at dusk on a cloudy night. Under the cover of darkness half of the remaining Elfin Army burst through the east wall. Under the confusion the army created in the enemy camp the civilians, young and old alike, escaped into the brush. The other half of the army aided the people out of the city then joined their brethren in the fighting. They would try to keep Stormy's men at bay to allow the refugees to get as far away as possible before joining them.

————◦◦◦◦◦————

"And that's when you showed up, sir. Did our scout not make it to Boman?"

"No," Dwarflord Boden said. "Perhaps he had been wounded and died on the way. We never saw him."

"Well, it looks like Typhon made it to Damek. You're proof of that," the captain said to Devlak who assured the captain the king and queen knew what was happening.

They had no more time for conversation. The fighting grew fierce and bloody. The rain ceased and gave the enemy a slight advantage. They hadn't counted on the fighting spirit of Merr and Derr. The Lunn brothers' two badgercats proved to be worth the equivalent of six men and were very much appreciated. The combined elf and dwarf armies slowed down the enemy's advances and gave the refugees half a days' head start to reach Boman. Over two thirds of the men in the combined army either perished or were badly wounded. The dead were left where they fell. The wounded were rushed to the front of the army away from the fray.

Devlak numbered with the wounded although he refused to retreat. Instead he fought beside his brethren thankful for the clouds. Five days later, the Elfin Nation, what was left of it, made it inside Boman with the combined army close behind and the doors were sealed against the enemy. They were safe. Or, so they thought.

Suddenly, an explosion rocked the Boman caverns and rock slides sealed them inside. No one knew how bad it was or how long it would be before help would come. They had enough food and supplies to last only eight months, and that was with careful rationing.

Quiet descended upon the people. They heard Stormy's men outside, marching away, and bearing southwest.

Someone had to get out the east portal. Two problems stood in the way. Dwarflord Boden explained to Devlak that it was an arduous journey and the portal was only large enough for the smallest to breach. He chose two of his smallest warriors to work their way to the outside. One was his faithful private. Someone had to let the elves and dwarves outside know their predicament. The dwarflord knew that was their only chance to see sunshine again.

———⁓⟋⟍⟋⟍⟋⟍⟋⟍———

"The refugees and then the army entered Boman on November 30," the private finished. "Stormy's army was close behind us having caught up during our trek there. After all were safe inside, we heard and felt a terrible explosion that rocked the entire cavern system. They chose myself and another to try and breach the narrow passage that led to the outside. I was the smallest and was able to make it out. My companion was not. He said he'd inform Dwarflord Boden I had made it. My job was to find either Dwarflord Ganesh or any of his clan and tell them what happened. Sire, by now, not much food is left for them."

"Our people and yours are trapped?" Avery asked.

"Yes, sire," the dwarf bowed. "May I ask a question?"

Avery nodded.

The private pointed. "Isn't that Stormy?"

"Angel defeated the enemy that was inside her," Barak answered. "She is now Alison. Remember that, private." Barak's eyes narrowed to slits as he continued. "I have a question for you. How do you know what was said to your dwarflord when the two armies met?"

The man stood straight. "I fight beside my dwarflord, sire. I'm his personal guard."

"I understand. Go and find yourself something to eat after attending to that arm. You're dismissed, private."

"Yes sir." He bowed and left.

"Alison, by any chance do you know what type of bomb was used?" Angel asked. "Was it nuclear?"

She shook her head. "I can't remember. I'm sorry."

"Or, won't," Serylda said under her breath.

Barak studied the ground in front of him. "Since we have to take a trip to Attor and then to Jasper, and as long as the Bomani people are safe inside, we'll let them be. With nearly half of the army heading to Boman to start the dig-out, they'll be in there for nine months, ten at the most. The people may feel on the verge of starving, but we'll have them free before then. And, we'll be able to talk to them through the walls.

So, they won't feel they're abandoned." He looked up when Cornellius coughed.

"Angel," Cornellius began, "Nicholas and I have an idea that may be of assistance to us all." At her nod, he continued. "With everyone's approval, he'll head out with the major and the army. They can drop off the children and Ariel at Damek if you so desire. I'd also like Rick to go. It's going to take them nearly thirty days of marching to reach Damek. So, I'd like the army to gather supplies while Nicholas rounds up some men. He can lead a group of Falconlanders to aid the dwarves."

"Thank you," Angel said and smiled. "I was going to suggest that very same thing. I would like to speak with Nicholas first. Since we're not sure what type of bomb was used, I'd like to teach him how to work the Geiger counter I've brought along. If it's safe, they can begin the dig-out immediately. If not, he can send someone to Damek to let us know as soon as we arrive."

"Yes," Barak agreed. "If it proves unsafe, the army can march to the east side of the caverns and enlarge the crack Rockwell squeezed out of."

While Angel went off to find Nicholas, Avery and Barak went to ready the army. Nicholas caught on quickly how the Geiger counter worked, much to Angel's surprise. By the time he had mastered the contraption, Avery had returned with the children, Ariel, and Rick in tow.

She hugged her offspring. "You both better behave this time and stay put at Damek."

"We promise," Jared said and backed away.

"We're sorry for the trouble we've caused," Janna said. "We've learned our lesson. We won't cause any more." She backed away, too.

"Good." Angel stood and sighed at the twins. "I already miss you both." She couldn't help herself and reached once more for the children. They rushed to her arms for another tight squeeze before she relinquished them to Ariel. Her children acted more mature than she wanted. They were growing up too fast, especially after the experience they endured. It was a hard lesson, one they would never forget. The six of them walked quietly to the head of the army where Barak shook Major Ironstone's hand.

"Good luck, major," they heard Barak say.

"We'll start the dig-out as soon as possible, sire. And, if it proves dangerous according to Nicholas..." He looked at Nicholas who nodded and smiled, then the major continued, "We'll concentrate our efforts on the east side of the cavern system and enlarge that air vent. In any case, I'll send a messenger to try and intercept you first at Krikor then at Damek to let you know of the plans."

"Very good, major." Barak stepped back.

The major mounted his horse and urged it next to Nicholas at the head of the army. Rick, Ariel and the twins rode behind them. The thirty five determined dwarf foot soldiers brought up the rear. Jamala waited between the horses the twins rode and the expanse to their left. With a wave, they headed northeast toward Falconland and beyond at the pace of a soldier's hike.

Avery placed an arm around Angel. She didn't hear him come up behind her. "Don't worry. They'll be fine," he reassured her. "I think they've really learned their lesson this time."

"I know." Angel sighed and wiped the tear running down her face. "I guess we should get going, too. We have about sixty to seventy days of foot travel ahead of us, according to Barak." She left his embrace when the last of the army passed by. Behind them, Barak sat astride his horse leading two others. Seth followed behind, never very far from the dwarf.

Once astride their own horses, Avery nodded his readiness to Barak. Niedra gathered the remaining wild badgercats and they ambled over to Angel's side. She patted the horse to calm it. The sight of a column of badgercats alongside her made her smile. She glanced over at Barak, sensing his eyes on her. He raised his eyebrows in question. She nodded. He understood. The cats, all of them, were going, too. Barak made the signal to move out, and the trek to Attor was underway.

"I sure wish we had enough horses for all my army to ride. It'd cut our travel time to about one month," Barak said as they made their way toward Attor. He glanced behind his shoulder at his forty doughty warriors.

"All we can do is get there as fast as is possible," Avery said.

"Either way, it's going to be a long trek without the children," Angel added.

Avery reached over and patted her hand. "All will work out."

———— ∾∾⧫∾⧫∾⧫∾∾ ————

One evening, sixty days into their journey, the company set up camp near the ancient salt lake. The five badgercats went off to hunt, as usual. Barak, with Avery's help, constructed the main campfire as Cornellius left with his falcons to hunt. Angel, Alison, and Serylda erected their tent. The men slept in the open, the norm for the dwarves. The women went to hunt for some vegetables for the evening's stew after their tent stood for the night. The army was left to hunt for their own food and settle down for the night. Being dwarves, the army was very resourceful.

Half an hour later, Cornellius returned with two rabbits, dressed and ready for the stew pot. The girls placed a container of water, with a few tubers added, to boil over the fire. After depositing the meat into the pot, the company of long-time friends sat either on the ground or on logs rolled next to the fire.

"Well, we should be at our destination in little over a week," Barak rasped.

"I for one will be glad to get there, do what we need to do, and leave," Alison added.

"Are you still having nightmares?" Barak asked.

"Yes." Alison sighed. More than once the company was awakened from Alison's nightmare screams.

"Perhaps a companion would help," Angel said. All eyes turned to her as she smirked. She pointed to two of the three remaining wild cats. "One of them wants to be your cat, dear sister. And, by the way, Serylda, the other wants to be yours."

Serylda laughed. "Why not. It seems Barak is doing okay with Seth."

"I'll try anything," Alison agreed.

Angel silently asked the two cats to join them. "This is Jakko, Alison. He told me he hears your nightmares and feels your terror when he does."

"Hello, Jakko," Alison said. She sat, a trance upon her face a moment before she spoke. "Wow, I can hear him in my mind. Very unnerving. But not uncomfortable. Thank you, sister, for introducing us to each other."

"And, Serylda, this is Gran." Angel gestured to the female. "She's been able to hear you ever since the cats had joined us."

Serylda just closed her eyes. "Yes, I agree," she said aloud.

"What did she say," Barak asked.

"She said to me, 'I am honored to be your cat'."

"Well, there's only one cat not paired. What does she tell you, Angel?" Barak wondered.

"She does not hear anyone except me at present. If she decides on someone, she will inform me. By the way, she told me her name is Zolia."

Cornellius interrupted them. "Supper is ready, if anyone is still hungry."

Everyone wasted no time to retrieve their bowls and helped themselves to food. After supper, they cleaned up and re-stoked the fire. Barak retrieved his pipe while Avery took out his flute. It had been a long while since Angel heard her husband play. She looked forward to the relaxation this night, though she dearly missed her children.

Before Avery put flute to mouth, the five cats gave a yowl. Suddenly, arrows flew through the air as thirty or so men charged into the camp. Ten dwarves were killed before the others, now armed, joined the fray. Ten more fell to the arrows before the fight ended. The badgercats cornered half a dozen intruders, all that was left. *My sisters and brothers want to kill them*, Niedra informed Angel.

Thank you for stopping them.

Please let us kill them, Jakko thought to Angel and Niedra

We need to talk to them, Jakko, Angel sensed to the cat.

At the same time, she heard Niedra tell him, *Listen to Angel. I want to kill, too. But, she is law.*

Angel's eyebrows rose. *I'm law?* she thought to herself. Aloud, she said, "Thank you, Niedra. And thank you, Jakko, for your concern. Please, thank your siblings for me."

Jakko growled and led the other cats away. Niedra stayed at Angel's side.

Avery and Barak joined her as she turned to the intruders.

"Who are you?"

They stood quiet.

"It does you no good to just stand here," Barak rasped. "We can still sic our cats upon you."

"How do you have control of them?" one asked.

"Just realize we do, and answer Angel's question," Avery said quietly.

Alison strode up. "Gordon, what are you doing here?" She looked over at Barak, adding, "This man was my second-in-command."

"Madam Stormy." The man who had spoken bowed. "We saw you in this dwarven scum company and thought you needed rescuing."

"I am no longer Stormy, Gordon. You are released from your obligation to commit war upon these people. Be at peace, as I am now."

"I don't understand."

"Do you not feel different around me?"

He frowned. "Well, yes. I no longer feel the rage and domination I felt in your presence."

"Good. There was an evil entity in control of me. It has been destroyed."

Avery placed a hand upon Alison's arm as he addressed the man, "If you are still loyal to this woman, please obey her. And, if you do, we shall let you go."

"You must promise me," Alison said, "that you will never fight against the people we've been at war with for so long."

"We vowed to obey *you*, my liege, years ago. That has not changed." All six men bowed at Alison. "We are honorable men and keep our vows no matter what. We remain at your service, my lady," Gordon said.

"We are traveling to Attor," Alison said. "Do you go with us?"

"Yes," Gordon agreed. "But we need to inform you of something, my liege. It concerns Attor." At Alison's nod, he continued, "Major Gaston will no longer listen to me. He has decided to raise an army of his own. By now, he has taken control of Attor. He is without honor. We were on our way to inform you, madam."

"This is news," Avery interjected. "With half our army killed in this fray, we have twenty six men, if we count these, to defeat this Gaston."

"He was one of my best fighters," Alison added. "And one with no remorse about killing. He enjoyed torturing his hostages."

Angel, Avery, and Barak moved to one side. Alison remained and asked Gordon questions concerning her former stronghold.

"We can have one or two cats guard these men tonight," Angel said. "In the meantime, I can covertly check each man's pledge to our cause, to be assured they will fight for us."

"Sound good to me," Barak agreed.

After informing the six men they were to help bury the twenty they killed, they were given a spot to rest. They were also told the cats would tear them up if they tried anything against their promises to behave. As they worked Angel silently and quickly assessed their mentalities and deemed them on their side.

Though they were men, they had fought like dwarves. Angel learned Cornellius had suffered a minor wound to his left arm. It didn't impair his ability to fight. All in all, she was thankful none of the major people in this struggle died. She curled up in her bag, and fell asleep knowing they slept safe in the presence of Niedra and her four siblings.

CHAPTER 10

More Answers

FIFTEEN DAYS LATER THE SQUAD reached the wastes of Attor. Good weather had followed them the entire trip. The earth seemed to know they were making things right and wanted to help. By the time they had made camp a half mile from the castle ruins, Angel was assured Stormy's men were loyal to Alison and the new order of things. They no longer thought of themselves as Stormy's army, but as Alison's troops. In the journey to Attor, Alison devised a plan that entailed two of her men to enter Attor and lure Gaston out.

Gaston sent one of the men back to Alison with a lethal gash in his side. He barely had enough life left to inform them Gaston knew of their plan, in Gaston's words, "to wipe us out."

"Looks like we have another battle on our hands," Cornellius said.

As they set up camp, Alison's men integrated themselves with the dwarf army, ready to do battle. On the trek to Attor, the men had made friends with the dwarves who accepted the new troops. The cats wandered the perimeter, the best guards in the company. Once while camp was being set up, Angel learned Jakko found a man but was unable to restrain himself and killed the man. He apologized and promised to try and exercise more control of himself next time.

That night when the women retired to their tent, Niedra stood guard outside. Avery and Barak remained by the campfire. Before Angel laid her head down, a commotion brewed outside the camp. The women, now armed, left the tent, and joined the battle. Angel used the quarterstaff she carried since before the children were born, the weapon given to her by Dwarflord Ganesh so long ago. Serylda carried a sword along with her quarterstaff. Alison retreated to squat next to a tree, having no weapon.

All was pandemonium, cats tearing and dwarves slashing and arrows swooshing through the air. In the middle of the battle, twenty elves joined the fray. When all was over, Angel learned only five dwarves and two men fell. Barak had suffered one gash to his right leg, enough to cause him to hobble. Angel tended the cut she received to her own cheek. She found her sister near the tree with an arrow in her left leg and one in her right forearm. As she ministered to Alison, she acknowledged the strangers who had joined the battle, the elves from Kaliborn. During the fray, there wasn't time to address them, only nod in their direction as they turned the tide to them in the battle.

Gordon, with sword in hand, brought the leader of the enemy army and his former friend, Gaston, to stand in front of Alison.

"You are a fool, Gaston," she told him as she watched Angel finish dressing her wounds. His snort turned her attention to him, her eyebrows raised in question.

"I laugh in your face, Stormy." He raised his chin. "I do not surrender. You have deserted us."

"Not I, Gaston. By raising an army against me, you broke your vow and are no longer an honorable man. You deserted *me*."

"Even so, I will die with my men." Suddenly overpowering Gordon, he grabbed the sword and fell upon it.

It happened so suddenly no one had time to stop the suicide. The twenty Kaliborn in attendance bowed their heads at his passing. The Kaliborn leader ordered a few of his elves to bury the man with his troops who died in the conflict. He then ordered others to bury their own along with the five dwarves and two men who fell in the battle. Then, he turned to Angel and Avery.

"I am King Selik Balen. We heard of the renegades in Attor and decided to root them out. We did not know you would be here also."

"I am glad you were, Selik," Avery said. "Else we'd had a harder time. I am Avery. And this is Angel."

Selik bowed. "We know who you are, Avery. When we were sent to Kaliborn, your mother, Kalika, was pregnant with you. Her last woman child, my wife, Lorina, awaits my return in Kaliborn with our son and his wife who is pregnant with our first grandchild. Regarding Angel. We heard rumors of the Alastrine savior, this savior of man, and knew she was successful fifteen years ago. We believed Angel to be this person."

"I am Barak, now Dwarflord of Jasper." Barak walked up and bowed his head at the Kaliborn leader.

Selik bowed and acknowledged the dwarf in return. "I presume Dwarflord Ganesh Blackstone has stepped down?"

"No. My father was killed in an ambush on November 18. I've been dwarflord since January 6, the day of my coronation and the day we left for Nemesis."

"I am sorry for your loss. We of the Kaliborn elves hope your reign is as great as was your father's."

"Thank you," Barak said with another bow. "I have a question for you. Why do you honor the one named Gaston like you do with our own warriors? Why do you not put them to flame?"

"We believe all life is sacred. So, we do honor to all alike, no matter friend or foe." Selik took a deep breath and added, "If this displeases you, we apologize."

"Excuse me," Angel interrupted. "We have one more task to perform before we need to return to the Great Crack. We need to check for certain chemicals inside Attor. Do you wish to aid us, Selik?"

"Yes."

"Then, you are welcome to share our fire," Barak added. "It is late. We will wait until morning to check out the stronghold."

The Kaliborn elves thanked Barak for his hospitality but set up their own tents a little away from the army. An hour later the area drew quiet as eyes were closed for the night. The cats kept vigilant watch throughout the night, the perfect sentries.

The next morning found the Kaliborn elves ready to aid in the search for the chemicals believed to be inside Attor. Once at the gate, ten of the thirty-five dwarves along with half the Kaliborn waited outside as the rest entered the ruins. Niedra and the cats also stayed outside to hunt since they weren't needed. Angel made sure they kept their senses alive for any enemy soldiers in the vicinity before letting them go. Now was not the time to be lax.

The squad worked in twos and threes. Angel chose Alison to accompany her. Barak took his sister and Avery opted for Cornellius. The thirty-five elves and dwarves paired off on their own with instructions to find one of the leaders if they discovered anything of importance.

"Don't disturb anything," Barak reminded them before letting them go.

Alison proved all but useless in finding the weapons. The longer she was herself and lived without the evil Zaxcellian entity, the more she forgot. Angel sensed her sister's quick return to normalcy and felt grateful for it. Alison's thoughts were becoming more herself, like she was just after they had left their native century. She kept the memories of the evil deeds forced upon her as Stormy but the alien thought patterns were fading. Angel was glad her sister wouldn't have to live with the mental animosity of the evil Zaxcellian.

Angel brought her thoughts back to the present. A couple of soldiers strode up to her. They found a passageway that led to a small room. Inside they had found several large piles of corroded iron shards, all that was left of four or five barrel-sized objects. On the way to the room, they met up with others and sent them to tell the rest of the warriors to retreat back outside. Avery and Cornellius trailed behind the girls, having caught up with them when they were also informed of the small room.

"That was it," Alison said, looking a little off-color. "I don't remember what was inside them but I do remember seeing four barrels in here. It's an old memory, when Ahriman was manipulated by the same evil that possessed me. But what was in them? I can't remember. I guess they corroded into nothingness." She frowned. "I wonder when that happened."

"We've got lucky, it seems," Cornellius said, as Barak and Serylda joined them.

"Not necessarily," Angel contradicted. "We don't know what was in them. It could have been the stuff Kalika warned us about."

"Is she still alive? Would she know?" Barak asked. "I thought you wanted to talk to the Ancient Ones as the first time you went into the Great Crack. I never thought beyond the idea that she'd still be alive."

"Yes, Kalika would know," Alison interrupted. "Ahriman and she were to be wed before Ahriman decided he wanted her for some other evil idea."

"You remember something of that?" Serylda asked, frowning.

Angel took hold of her friend's arm sensing trouble. "If there is any truth in that, Kalika will tell us if she so wishes. And, yes," Angel looked at Barak, "Kalika is still alive."

"I guess the next stop is the Great Crack and then to Jasper," Barak said.

"We won't join you," Selik interrupted behind them. "We are traveling back to our home now that the renegades have been dealt with."

"Are you sure you wouldn't like to see Kalika?" Angel asked.

"Thank you, no. Just give her our respects."

"When we have dug our comrades out and rebuilt Krikor, we shall make a trip to visit you," Angel promised.

"We await your arrival, my lady." King Selik bowed low.

The company made their way back out of Attor. After saying a thankful "goodbye" to the Kaliborn elves, they turned and the new trek to the Great Crack ensued.

Angel did a quick computation. It was April 22 and it would take another thirty days to reach the Great Crack. In her heart she hoped Barak was right about the people in Boman. A few months of no food would be very hard on anyone in those caves. She hoped they would ration the food before it became critical for them. Still, she knew her own people well. They would rather die of starvation than take the scarce food from another culture even if they were gladly invited to stay, albeit involuntarily.

Tomorrow Angel was going down into the Great Crack for her fourth time. It was now May 20, and she was thankful that the time had passed so quickly and uneventfully. Barak had camp set up at the same place they had originally used on her first trip down so many years ago. Angel felt at home here now. It was getting so familiar. She felt anticipation grow inside her at the prospect of again seeing the old king and queen.

The next morning, in the tent she shared with Serylda and Alison, Angel felt the familiar sensation her crystal sent out whenever it was in the presence of the Centauri in the caves nearby. In sudden insight, she held the warm crystal in her hands and concentrated upon it. The queen's voice was barely discernable. She was right. Somehow she used the crystal to hear the old queen's thoughts. After a few more tries, the thoughts were loud enough for Angel to make out the words.

Hello, Angel.

Hello, my queen, she thought with a smile. *How is this possible?*

Please, Angel. You don't need to address me as queen. Just use mother or Kalika. Either one will do. I'd like to say I'm glad you've figured out how to use your crystal to talk to me. It is how we used those crystals in our own world. But, right now, I know you're not alone. Who is with you?

Avery, Barak, and Serylda, among others, are here. May I come see you?

Stay where you are. We are both coming to you. Iomar wants to surprise Avery so don't let on he is coming up, too.

Angel's smile grew. *I'll keep his secret and let the others know you are on your way.*

Angel left the tent quietly, allowing Alison to sleep. It was still dark. Serylda stood by the fire with Avery and Barak. Like her sister, everyone else was still asleep. She smiled, glad her friend and her sister had acted civil to each other on the trip.

Serylda caught sight of Angel before she reached them. Getting another mug she poured Angel some coffee and sat down with her on a nearby log. She handed Angel the extra mug and drank from her own.

"Thank you," Angel said and took a sip. "Mm, that is good. Barak's doing, I'll wager."

Serylda nodded and smirked. "Of course, who else brews such good tasting coffee?"

"Everyone is sure quiet this morning. What's up?"

"We're trying to decide what to do next," Avery answered. "We've been impatiently waiting for you to join us."

"We do nothing at the moment," Angel informed them. "I'm to let you all know Kalika is coming up." She smiled at their expressions. "I used my crystal to talk to her, something that wasn't revealed to me until now." Looking at her husband, she added, "Your mother told me we're to stay right here. I'll send Niedra to help find our location when she reaches the rim."

"I hope you've told her that," Barak stated.

Angel paused looking skyward then back at Barak. "Don't worry my dear dwarf. Kalika knows. In fact, I've just asked Niedra to collect her."

Barak turned in time to see the big cat disappear over the rim.

Cornellius joined them carrying his own mug. "What's up?" he asked as he poured himself some coffee. With pot in hand and looking at each of them, he offered to refill their mugs. After doing that and returning the pot to the fire, he took a seat next to Angel.

Avery beamed and said, "We're going to have company. My mother is joining us."

Fifteen minutes passed and the sky began to lighten for the coming day. When Avery started pacing everyone smiled at his anticipation. He kept looking toward the canyon only to return to his pacing. Five more minutes passed and he grew restless. He turned his back to the canyon. At the same time, everyone's smile grew broader as they beheld Niedra coming over the rim followed by Kalika and Iomar. Apparent to all, the couple was in excellent health, neither one out of breath from their climb, though Kalika looked as old as Iomar now.

Avery frowned at his friends and faced his wife. "Well, when is she going to be here?" He threw his arms wide.

"Right now, my son," his father said behind him as he spun in shocked surprise.

He laughed. "I hadn't expected to see you, father. I'm tickled to see you both. I've missed you so much." He gave each a big bear hug, starting with his mother.

"You look good, son," Iomar said, holding Avery away from him. He looked over the gathering. More and more were joining them. One especially caught his eye. "And who is this?"

"That is Stormy," Serylda said, then corrected herself. "Forgive me. She is Alison, Queen Angel's twin sister."

Alison slowly joined the gathering. Angel felt the anxiety she harbored and sent a quick thought to the old queen. *She needs compassion and understanding. She's nervous.*

I understand, Kalika thought back.

"Hello, my child." Kalika held out her hand. "You may not remember me but I, however, remember you. I can sense you're not as wild as you used to be, which, my dear," she said as she leaned toward Alison, "is a good thing."

Alison took the hand that promised acceptance and forgiveness. "No, ma'am. I don't and I'm not. I want to thank you for believing in me. I can see it in your eyes and feel it in your touch."

"My queen," Angel interrupted. "May I ask a favor of you?" At Kalika's nod, she continued, "Can you tell if Alison suffered any damage from the Zaxcellian's control and possession of her?"

"Yes, I believe I can." She motioned Alison nearer. "I should not be able to hurt you. If I do, please forgive me."

"What do I do?" Alison asked.

"Just stand quietly." Kalika placed her right hand on Alison's head and closed her eyes. After a few moments, she stepped back and allowed her arms to fall to her sides. "I sensed no residual intelligence in your mind. I believe you are completely free of the alien and are once again yourself."

Alison hung her head. "No, I'm not. I've kept the memories of the evil deeds I've done while I was Stormy. It shames me to know the hurt I've caused."

"You must forgive yourself. You were not in control. And, in time, everyone will agree with me." Kalika gave Alison a gentle motherly hug. "Be at peace, child."

Alison looked into the Centauri's ancient eyes and knew all was well. She accepted the advice to heart.

Angel gently took her from Kalika and hugged her. "I'm glad for you, sister."

"Excuse me," Barak interrupted. "Before we get to the real reason we're here, let's all get comfortable. I'll make more coffee while Cornellius hunts up two more mugs."

After Iomar and Kalika were each given a seat and mugs were filled with fresh coffee, everyone gathered around. The thirty five dwarves stood behind and listened in.

Angel glanced around at everyone then addressed Kalika. "We found a few metallic canisters in Attor. They've deteriorated and their contents are gone. Alison couldn't remember what they were, only that they were some kind of doomsday weapon from your homeworld. Do you have any idea what she meant?"

"First," Kalika said, "answer me this. What did the countryside look like around Attor compared with fifteen years ago?"

"More desolate, to me," Angel answered.

"I agree," Serylda added. "It was barren rock. No plant or animal life survives within ten miles of the fortress."

"No further?"

Serylda shook her head.

Kalika drew in a deep breath and slowly let it escape before answering. "If it's what I think, then it's the reason Attor is so desolate and will stay that way for a millennium. It sounds like a plant biologic from Centaurus."

"You'll have to explain what a plant biologic is to those of us who've never heard of such a thing," Barak interrupted.

Alison spoke before anyone else. "Biologics are types of chemicals that attack undesirable growths, kills them and keeps other things from growing in the area they've been used. People had used such things for the control of weeds, insects, and other unwanted living things. They were called fungicides, herbicides, and insecticides."

"These particular biologics would be worse than anything made here," Kalika added. "They were intended to be used on an uninhabitable planet. But, since we landed here, we didn't need them. Ahriman must've transported some down from our ship before making his ultimatum. When this particular type of biologic is used sparingly, if it's what I think, it acts as a super fertilizer. If it's used full strength, it can become a weapon."

"Excuse me," Angel interrupted. "Is this the same doomsday weapon you told me about? You know, the one meant to protect others from the Centauri?"

"Yes," Kalika answered.

"Then, what's this about it being intended for an uninhabited planet? Didn't it need Centauri DNA to activate it?"

"And how is it supposed to protect us from you?" Barak added.

"I will answer your question later, Barak. First, for now, Angel, what you say is true. Since you've told me about the corroded containers and the absence of any life around Attor, the presence of this biologic would explain all."

"I'm confused," said Cornellius.

"So am I," said Serylda. "How is it a weapon?"

Kalika took a sip of coffee. "In large quantities, it destroys the soil bacteria, sterilizing it for about a hundred years, long enough for someone to introduce different bacteria. Without bacteria in the soil, plants, then animals die. Of course, this takes time. But in large enough quantities, it will destroy all life. Even the Centauri."

"That's what you believe happened in and around Attor." Barak shook his head.

"Yes, if it's this biologic I spoke of."

"Okay," Angel agreed. "Now, what about the need for Centauri DNA to start the reaction?"

"I believe Ahriman may have used some of his own blood to test it. Since the canisters didn't survive the years, their contents gradually added to the experiment and kept it going until it reached the outside."

Angel thought a moment. "That's why Attor looks worse today than back then. Does nothing stop it?"

"Eventually it quits, when the reaction can no longer sustain itself. Which I believe has happened since the devastation is within the ten miles surrounding Attor." Kalika looked at Barak. "Now, to answer your question about how it protects you. We always saved enough to ingest. It works on our bodies, completely consuming them. It leaves no trace of our DNA to contaminate any world we deem threatened by us. And, yes, we know exactly how much is needed for the job."

"I didn't mention this before," Alison interjected, "but when we were inside Attor, I began feeling ill." Angel recalled that her sister looked a little below par inside Attor.

Kalika nodded. "That proves my theory. It definitely was the biologic. It was working on you."

"Why didn't it make the rest of us feel sick?" Serylda asked, still not convinced. "I know I felt fine. Still do." Everyone that had been inside the ruins nodded in agreement.

"It builds up in your system and stays there," Kalika explained. "That's how it kills. Since Alison has lived there for a while, she's been exposed to it and can never return there."

"Kills?" Alison asked, alarmed. "Am I in peril?"

"No," Kalika patted her arm, reassuring her. "As long as you never return there, you'll be fine. You won't grow worse but your health will never be the same."

Barak turned to Alison. "Do you recall if Stormy used something like that at Krikor or Boman?"

Alison shook her head. "That is one thing I wish I could remember. I'm sorry."

Angel rose. "Well, it looks as if the only way to get that answer is to travel to Krikor and see for ourselves."

"Yes," Barak agreed. "And then on to Boman."

"We should leave now," Serylda said, and stood. "It's just now midday. We could be a dozen miles closer to Krikor by nightfall if we leave within the half hour."

All agreed and fifteen minutes later, the company was once again under way. Their number had grown by two. The old queen and king decided to accompany them the entire way. Angel and Barak had misgivings but Kalika assured all they were in excellent health. Nevertheless, they were given horses, and the trek continued.

That evening they had left the Great Crack thirteen miles behind them. Barak, impressed with their speed, glanced over at Angel and nodded. She read the confidence and acceptance he had shown for the old couple. Iomar and Kalika were given the girls' tent. Angel, Alison, and Serylda made their bedrolls out under the stars with the men. After supper, everyone settled near the fire. As before, Barak made his delicious coffee for all to enjoy. When everyone sat with full mugs in hand, Avery posed a question to his mother.

"Were you and Ahriman betrothed?"

She smiled. "Yes, a long time ago. We were to be married after our people settled on our new home."

"Which never happened," Barak added.

"Exactly," Kalika assured all. "We ended up stranded here due to Ahriman's betrayal, or rather his control by the Zaxcellian. Because of that, our engagement was voided by our leaders after I requested a termination of betrothal, which had never happened before."

"I have a question." Cornellius took a drink from his mug before posing his query. "Since you broke your engagement, why didn't Ahriman kill you? He had no ties to you after that."

"I know why," Alison piped up. Everyone focused upon her. She looked over at Kalika, then down in sudden embarrassment.

"Go ahead, my child," Kalika gently encouraged.

"Ahriman had such a love for you, it affected the evil Zaxcellian to the point it kept that love for you even when it had possession of me." Alison looked directly at Kalika and continued. "That is one memory I still retain due to the intensity of it."

Angel grunted once. "The love for Kalika was so strong and the Zaxcellian possessed Ahriman for such a long time, that Ahriman's love became a part of it. At least you have one good memory of your dreadful encounter, sister."

"Sounds logical to me," Iomar said, covering his mouth and trying to hide the yawn.

Avery noticed his father's fatigue. "I suggest we better turn in. We still have a long way to go."

———✦———

The trek to Krikor went without mishap. With Angel's control, the badgercats kept them informed of any obstacles in their way. The weather stayed nice even though they were fully into spring's rainy season. The air grew warmer the closer they traveled to their goal. The trees slowly put on their greenery. The rains stayed ahead of them, freshening the air. They avoided the area around the evil city of Amar. Other than that, their course stayed straight toward their goal of Krikor.

As it turned out, it was July 15 before they reached the wastes of the elfin city, good weather or not. Angel signaled the cats to begin their hunt for possible survivors. She realized it was a long shot but couldn't help herself. She had to know beyond doubt, even though she sensed no one in the rubble.

"My beautiful city is gone." A stunned Kalika stood in the middle of what was once the castle courtyard.

"Stormy's men did a thorough job of razing this city," Alison added. No longer did she think of herself as Stormy. She left that association behind sometime during their trek to Krikor. She forgave herself and embraced her old name with confidence. It helped that Kalika had accepted her as Alison at the Great Crack. Taking Kalika's lead, the others also accepted her as Alison and no longer as Stormy.

The Centauri placed a gentle hand on Alison's shoulder. The stunned look on the old woman's face faded. "He couldn't kill me but he hurt me most in this fashion. I'm glad you don't blame yourself now."

Angel joined the two women. A tear ran down her cheek. "I didn't get the chance to live here long. But in the time I did, I grew to love this city."

Avery spoke up from behind them. "We still have our lives. We can rebuild Krikor better than before. But, right now we can't do anything. The Bomani people, along with our own, need our immediate help."

"Yes," interrupted Barak. "I speak for all my brethren, Jasper and Bomani dwarves all, when I say once Boman is again free, the Elfin Nation will have all our support to rebuild Krikor."

Angel sighed and faced the two men. "You're both correct. We should leave immediately. We could be there in a matter of days."

Barak nodded. "The dig-out should be nearly finished by now. And, I'm anxious to get my hands dirty." He rubbed his hands in anticipation.

"Yes," Avery teased. "Why should the army get all that nice hard work?"

"Exactly," Barak grinned back.

Everyone laughed. Angel reveled in the light banter in spite of the devastation surrounding them. It was a good sign and cheered her up immediately.

The company waited five more minutes for the cats to finish their task. They howled to each other as they did their work. When they fell silent, Niedra, standing next to Angel, let out a blood-curdling screech that had everyone ready for a nonexistent battle.

Angel looked sheepishly at her comrades and apologized amid the sound of weapons being sheathed. "Sorry. I should've warned you. Niedra was just calling the other cats back here. She says the city is completely deserted, so we may as well head for Boman now."

Ten minutes passed before they began the final leg of their journey. The wild cats took up positions ahead of the squad. Their tails twitched with excitement.

Angel felt the enjoyment of the day. Ignoring the destruction surrounding her, she concentrated on her environment and saw what the cats did. Even with the charring the city received, sprouts broke through the ashes everywhere she looked. Life was already returning to the beloved city. She pointed out several areas to the old queen and king and felt their gratitude in her head. *Barak was right,* she thought. *We'll rebuild this city better than before, and Mother Nature has already begun doing it for us.*

They followed the path the refugees had taken in their rush to Boman. Even Angel had no trouble following it. Bodies from both sides of the skirmish lay rotting along the way. Each time they came across one, Barak had a couple of his men bury the body. They arrived at Boman on August 4. Major Dag Ironstone strode up, a huge grin on his dark face. After the carnage on the trail, it was a welcomed sight to Angel.

"This is one person very glad to see you, sire. Nicholas had checked for radiation as instructed by Queen Angel. And as I hope you already know, all was clear and I ordered the troops to begin the dig-out immediately. That's when we heard Devlak's signal. Everyone who survived the attack is fine, albeit a little hungry. The elves helped in devising a plan to make their food last in case they ended up trapped for a long period of time."

Barak laughed heartily and pounded the major on his back and knocked him off balance. "Excellent, my friend. How much longer before we gain entry?" Angel was grateful Barak had the major in charge. Dag Ironstone was Jasper's quarry master and knew everything there was to know about working stone.

The major grinned. "I estimate we should be done around the fourteenth of this month."

Barak's eyebrows shot upward. "That soon? You get it done by then and I'll make you a colonel."

"Yes, sire." Major Dag stole a quick look at Cornellius standing next to Barak. "The Falconlanders have helped a lot in this endeavor. They have proven themselves a stout people despite their soft homeland."

"Soft, yes, but deadly, too." Nicholas quietly laughed and strode up to stand beside his uncle.

Barak grabbed Nicholas by his arms. "Well met, my friend. Let's find some coffee and you can tell us of your trek here." After dismissing the troops, Barak nodded at Ironstone and the major led the three to fresh brewed coffee.

"Okay," Nicholas began, "looks like a lot has happened since I left. And, Barak? Is Seth still with you?"

"He's with Niedra." Barak harrumphed. "It appears the cats definitely 'hear' certain people." He chuckled. "I'm still in awe about it."

Angel watched them amble away after the promised coffee. She wondered what they talked about but refrained from invading their minds. She sighed and turned to her husband. "I miss the kids."

"Me, too." He took her by the arm and pulled her along. "Let's go for a stroll and get away from everyone for a little while."

Alison let them know she wanted to stay and visit with Kalika and Iomar. Angel smiled at her sister, glad she looked well. They missed the smiles and nods Avery's parents exchanged as they walked off.

CHAPTER 11

Boman

THIRTY MINUTES LATER, ANGEL AND Avery strode up to the cook wagon and asked for two mugs of coffee. They enjoyed their short walk and was anxious to hear how the twins fared. They joined the four men next to a warm fire. Barak and Cornellius sat opposite Nicholas and Dag. Barak rose and helped Avery position another log next to the fire. Angel and Avery sat on it and listened in.

Avery took a sip of his coffee, and looking at Barak, said, "That hits the spot. Almost as good as mine." He winked at Angel and grinned at the other's expression. She glanced down.

"Has everyone else retired?" Avery asked, changing the subject.

Barak nodded. "I was about to listen to Dag's and Nicholas's story when I saw you two. Figured you'd like to hear it, also."

"Thanks," Angel said. "We do."

"Well," Nicholas began, "it was pretty much uneventful."

———————

Nicholas mounted his horse and nudged her into motion. Gaining position at the head of the army, he placed the twins, Ariel, and Rick behind himself. He nodded at Major Dag who gave the signal to move out.

He could keep a better watch over the twins if they rode just behind him. He hoped they would behave themselves on their journey back to Falconland. He wasn't going to allow them to embarrass him again. Twice in one lifetime was enough. At least he had Ariel to help him control the children. All seemed well, so far.

The army had traveled for about three hours when he decided he grew tired of the silence coming from behind him. "Are you three going to sulk all day?"

"No, sir," Janna answered quietly, her voice barely above a whisper. She sounded on the verge of tears. Ariel patted her arm in sympathy.

He sighed and turned his attention on Jared. "And what about you, my young man?"

"I wish we could've stayed with mom and dad," he mumbled.

Ariel reached over and, like she had done with Janna, patted his arm. "You know where they were going. You also know it's too dangerous for us."

"I'd still like to have seen Attor," the boy said, stubbornly.

Nicholas thought a moment. "Tell you what, Jared. You, too, Janna. If you both behave all the way to Damek, and stay there this time, I'll take you to see the area when I turn twenty-five. Of course, it all depends on your parents' approval."

Jared looked up and slowly smiled. "Agreed."

"Janna?"

She glanced at her twin. Then, setting her gaze upon Nicholas, she nodded. She wiped the tears from her face and beamed. With that, Ariel started educating the twins on their immediate environment.

Nicholas turned back to the front. He pulled the Geiger counter out of his saddlebag and started studying it. He relied on Ariel to keep the twins occupied.

Rick urged his horse forward and joined Nicholas. "Do you still remember how to use that?"

"Yes," he answered. "I never knew man could be so evil."

"I agree. Why would man consider playing with something so destructive as nuclear devices? It seemed to me we're the only persons who understood Queen Angel. I caught on when she explained it at Jasper."

"Maybe it's because we're not set in our ways, you and I. You know, not as old."

Rick nodded. "Perhaps. I wonder if Ariel understands it. We should bring the subject up after the kids are put to bed tonight."

"Great idea."

That night after Ariel had tucked the kids into bed, they sat around a small fire.

"Well," Ariel informed them, "the children fell right to sleep."

"I want to discuss this radiation business with you two," Nicholas began. He showed them how the Geiger counter worked. After his demonstration, both Ariel and Rick sat back, Ariel in shock.

"I never knew man could be so evil," Ariel whispered, repeating what Nicholas had said to Rick earlier that day. "Why would such weapons be made?"

"Who cares?" Rick said, gazing at Ariel. "We have to live with the consequences now."

She gazed back at him.

His voice, suddenly a little harsh, Nicholas said, "At one time, according to Queen Angel, man used this radiation for good."

"How?" Ariel asked, her attention back on him.

"She said they used to be able to look into the body using radiation. They could see broken bones and certain diseases."

"Wow," Rick said, awed. "I sure would like to know how they did that." He turned his eyes to the Geiger counter in Nicholas's hands. "Even so, I never imagined something so devastating as this nuclear bomb and the radiation accompanying such a thing. Why would man invent such an evil thing? I wonder, did radiation play a part in the Ancients coming to earth? I know they brought Angel to this time; that she was from the past, a past vastly different than we know. But to know the marvels of the twentieth century. Wow."

Nicholas agreed. "I know she mentioned that radiation could be used for good or bad. But when she described the side effects, it's hard for me to see it more than just too dangerous, especially if this Geiger counter and its use are anything to go by." He laid the device on the ground next to his feet.

Ariel nodded. "I remember once she had told me about electricity. Did you know lightning is a form of electricity? It baffles me how the ancient ones manipulated that energy. How in the world did one harness lightning? It sounds more like magic. And I know there's no such thing as magic."

Nicholas sighed. "It's silly for us to keep wondering about those ancient marvels. Besides, we've been given an ancient marvel to detect an ancient poison."

"It's a little frightening," Ariel said.

Nicholas pretended bravery he didn't feel. "I hope with all my being that when the time comes, we'll be able to use this contraption correctly."

———⁓⁓∾∾⟳⟲∾∾⁓⁓———

As the days passed and the army drew near Damek, Nicholas talked to Ariel and Rick about this danger. It kept them up most nights. They obsessed about the subject.

The night of March 2 found the company at their last campsite before entering Damek. Everyone had retired for the night except the first five sentries. Nicholas kept watch near camp while the other four sentries had perimeter watch.

The night was clear with a full moon shining down on the camp. Ariel couldn't sleep so she left the tent she shared with the children. She found Nicholas a few yards outside the campfire's glow. He sat quietly on a dry log.

"Can't sleep?" he asked. He patted the spot next to him. "Have a seat." As she did so, he continued, "I'll be glad when we enter Damek tomorrow. But now, I want to thank you for your help with the twins. And myself." He smiled. "I don't feel so overwhelmed with this radiation responsibility thrust upon me now, thanks to you."

She smiled back. "I know." She took one of his hands into her own. "I have a confession to make and I feel this is the last chance I'll get to tell you." She paused. He looked over at her and she returned his gaze. "I'm in love with you, Nicholas."

He took a deep breath, thankful for her boldness. "Somehow I'd hoped you'd tell me that. I'm in love with you, too."

He kissed her softly then held her close. She leaned her head on his shoulder. They sat like that enjoying each other's company until Janna called out from the tent fifteen minutes later.

"I guess I'd better go." Ariel rose and sighed.

Nicholas rose too, and gave her one more kiss before letting her go. "Goodnight," he whispered in her ear. His relief showed up half an hour later and he made his way to his bedroll. It was the first time in a long time he fell asleep with a smile on his face.

The next day around noon, they stood in front of Damek's gates waiting for them to open. Once they did, Nicholas nodded at Ariel. She led the children through followed by the dwarf army. Major Dag and

Rick waited alongside Nicholas. After the last soldier entered, Nicholas gave the major the name of the person to see for supplies. Rick knew the man to see and said he'd go with Dag. Nicholas advised them to get some rest afterward, making sure the army did, too.

On March 4, the dwarf army was restocked and well-rested, ready to begin the Boman dig-out. Accompanying the dwarves were forty Falconlanders. Nicholas sat proudly atop his horse and surveyed his combined army as they waited for him outside the city's gates, ready for him to lead them north.

The twins and Ariel stood near the gate. He glanced over at them. Suddenly, in a burst of bravado and not caring what others thought, he dismounted, strode over to them and grabbed Ariel. He gave her a kiss that left them both breathless and whispered to her, "dream of me." He let her go and the twins whooped with glee. Laughing, he tousled their hair and admonished them to behave.

Without looking back he remounted his horse and urged it forward ahead of Major Dag and Rick. Now at the head of the column, he raised his right fist and abruptly brought it down. The trek to Boman was underway once more.

It took them a little over a month to draw near Krikor. They didn't waste a lot of time and continued on toward Boman. Twenty miles from the caverns, he started checking for radiation as instructed. Wanting to be thorough after what Angel had told him about the dangers, it took three days to travel the distance. To the army's relief, he detected no radiation.

After setting up camp, he called for a meeting. Major Dag and his three lieutenants joined Nicholas and Rick at the main campfire. Two Falconlanders were also present, Daryn Barnes and Geof Dakota. Discussion focused on the dig-out and sending word to Angel and the others of their progress.

———◦◦◦◦◦◦———

"And that's it, sir," Nicholas finished. "We arrived here on April 25 and began working the next day. Barnes and Dakota are captaining our troops. And all are under Major Ironstone's command."

Angel sensed Nicholas didn't tell them everything. She decided to keep quiet and mention it to Cornellius later. She sent a silent message to Avery about it.

"Sounds good," Barak commented.

"Good indeed." Cornellius slapped Nicholas on the back. "I'm very proud of you. You've proven yourself. Now I have another task for you. I want you to go back to Damek for more supplies and men. Head for Krikor from Damek. We should be done here by then and will meet you there."

"If we arrive before you, sir, we'll start the clean-up in preparation for the rebuild." Nicholas rose. "I'm going to take Rick with me, if that's okay." When he received a nod of agreement from Avery, he bowed. "I'll get ready to leave now."

Angel laid a hand on his arm. "Do me a favor. Bring the twins and Ariel back with you. They can help with some things, too."

"Yes, ma'am." Nicholas bowed to all and left.

"Cornellius, may we speak with you?" Avery asked.

The others left the three alone. Angel and Avery sat on the now empty spaces on the logs.

"What's on your minds?"

Avery glanced at Angel who answered. "Did you know Nicholas is in love?"

"No." Cornellius's eyebrows rose. "You know who it is. Am I right?"

Angel nodded and smiled at his sudden insight. "It's Ariel. I sensed something between them at Nemesis. Just now I sensed it has grown into love. I think something happened on their trek to Damek that Nicholas left out. And I think it happened on their last night on the trail."

Avery laughed. "Then what I overheard earlier from several of the soldiers makes sense. He kissed Ariel in front of everyone before they left Damek."

Cornellius thought a moment, then laughed heartily. "I've just decided on the perfect gift for him. Since I've acquired two falcons recently, I'll let him have one, his choice. He won't know, of course, until they wed. I'll have him help me train them for both our hand and voice." He drew in a deep breath and released it before continuing. "Of course, I may need your help to keep him in the dark, Angel. Do you think you can talk to the falcons and make them understand?"

Angel raised her left hand to cup her chin. "I can try. You realize they're not as intelligent as the badgercats and that I've never done this with other animals, but I'll do what I can." She shook her finger at him. "My friend, you can be pretty sneaky at times."

The three friends laughed so heartily they drew stares from the others nearby. Niedra padded up and softly mewed. Angel sensed the gladness the animal felt to see her mistress in a good mood.

Ten days passed, only two of those days were dry. The off-and-on rain did little to hamper the dig-out. In fact, it pushed the dwarves to work harder. A yell went up and one dwarf ran to tell the news. They were about to break through.

Major Dag strode up to the fire. Sitting round it was Cornellius, Avery, Angel, Serylda, Barak, and Alison. They knew the time grew near for the break-through and wanted to witness it when it happened. Iomar and Kalika wanted to witness the event, too. Angel left to inform them. They agreed to meet at the worksite.

She reached over and petted Niedra who strode beside her.

So, you want to be a part of this.

Yes. Brothers and sisters do, too. I told them we make man nervous. So, they stay away.

Nervous? You learn new words easier now. Angel chuckled. Avery glanced her way. She nodded toward the cat. He smiled back in understanding.

I heard word from man yesterday.

I'm glad you're here, my dear friend. Let me ask Avery a question.

"Niedra has informed me that the other cats want to be at the break-out, also. What do you think?"

Avery grinned. "I don't see why not. They've shown their loyalty to us. I think Barak would allow it. But, I also think we'd better warn him and the others first."

"I agree." *Niedra, I'll let you tell the others they can come. But they need to stay with us until we let the men know.*

Niedra thought nothing, only purred her agreement. She rubbed against Angel's arm as the other cats started gathering around her and Avery. The sun peeked through a break in the clouds. Angel took hold of her husband's hand as they continued toward the cave entrance, the cats, all five of them, following with Niedra leading the animals.

The entourage arrived at the cave entrance five minutes later. Angel studied the crowd. She watched the mixture of elves, dwarves, and men milling about in harmony. She grinned when a murmur started in the back of the assembly where they were. People gave way to them, the cats strolling behind. She sensed no fear from the crowd. Instead she felt the acceptance and noticed smiles on their faces as they watched the animals. *That is good*, she thought.

Barak looked around noticing the quiet commotion and spotted the cats following Angel and Avery. Angel didn't need to alert him of the animals' wish to be at the breakout. He smiled at her. At the same time, Seth 'told' Angel he had asked his master if they could be present. Barak had agreed. After the cats took positions a few paces behind her, the crowd grew quiet.

At the entrance, Dag Ironstone motioned for Barak to join him. Both dwarves were given the honor of removing the last huge boulder. They leaned their bodies against the obstacle, and began to shove the great boulder.

But before anything happened, a shout went up behind the gathering. The badgercats left Angel's side in a rush for the commotion. From Niedra Angel learned a band of men were attacking. Nobody had any warning so no one was armed. A handful of the workers were killed by the attackers before the cats fell upon them with a vengeance. None of the assailants survived.

Angel and Alison were the first to arrive at the carnage.

"They were Stormy's assassins," Alison said. "This one was the worst of the men in her legion."

"It looks like a couple of the men who agreed to never fight us joined this faction," Angel added. She recognized two of the dead men.

"This man was Gaston's right hand man." Alison pointed to one of the bodies. "Perhaps he heard of the skirmish at the stronghold in Attor and decided vengeance upon us for that."

Barak assigned five men to bury the remains. Angel "thanked" the cats for their willingness to protect the crowd even though they left none of the attackers alive to question. The rest of the gathering returned to the cavern entrance. Angel sensed the crowd's more somber mood after the loss of the workers. She hoped the release of the people inside the caverns would bring back the happy atmosphere of earlier.

Once again Barak and Dag Ironstone took their place beside the massive boulder and with a great heave shoved the giant rock sideways. Slowly, the rock gave way to the great strength of the dwarves' determination. All fell silent as they backed away. Several others rushed up and removed the remaining boulders completely exposing the cavern's opening.

Angel hurried to the opening for her turn. Avery followed and stood beside her. She shouted into the black hole, "Come out and enjoy the fresh air once more!"

A shout went up as the dwarves and elves inside Boman slowly stepped out, squinting into the afternoon sun, now in a partly cloudy sky. The date was August 14. They were finally free after nearly nine months of entrapment. As they exited the caverns, each elf gave Angel and Avery a hug and Barak a nod of thanks, the freed dwarves just nodded. At the sight of the five huge cats, the liberated souls hesitated for just a moment. Seeing the calm demeanor of the animals and the crowd surrounding the cats, they knew all was well. Besides, they had lived with two badgercats and were used to them. Several dwarves and elves took groups of the hungry people to longed-for meals.

Two hours later, DwarfLord Greyrock and Devlak exited the caverns, the last of the entombed individuals. They left with Barak to discuss dwarf business. The Lunn brothers, who came out ahead of the two dwarves, were followed by their cats.

"Queen. King," they said in unison and bowed. The cats mewed and rubbed against Niedra, who purred back.

"They are quite happy to be out of that tomb," Merwyn said.

"They want to hunt," Derwyn said.

"And, they should," Avery said. "I think they're getting too smart." He laughed when all three cats gave a screech followed by the other cats present. With Angel's nod at Niedra, the entire cat pack left with Niedra leading.

"By the way," Angel interrupted, "How did they act cooped up in there?" She motioned back toward the cave entrance.

"It was a bit trying at first," Merwyn began.

"After the first day, they realized they were in the same fix as we were," Derwyn continued.

"After they learned of the small opening in the east leading to the outside, they used it for escaping and hunting every third day," Merwyn added.

"They don't have to return inside so they're very happy now," Derwyn said.

Angel, getting dizzy from the familiar way the two talked, interrupted them, "So, they fared better than the people?"

"Yes, ma'am," they said in unison and grinned. They knew how they affected her.

Barak, Devlak, and Boden sauntered up. All three wore smiles. Boden gave Angel and Avery a deep bow.

"I thank you most deeply for finally ending the Ahriman threat from the lands. Dwarflord Barak has informed me of all the happenings these long months had brought. With all the skills my people possess, we shall aid you and your people in rebuilding Krikor."

"Perhaps making it more magnificent than before," added Barak.

"Thank you, Dwarflord Boden." Angel bowed back. "We accept your offer most graciously."

The old queen and king of Krikor nodded at Boden. He reciprocated their move. They had stood quietly behind Angel and Avery during the entire time the trapped people had been exiting Boman.

"And, now my news," Devlak began. When all were attentive, he continued, "I've fallen in love with Dwarflord Boden's only daughter, Raven. Both her parents have already given their consent." He laughed at Angel's astonishment. "Yes, I'm finally getting married, too."

Avery laughed and swatted the dwarf heartily on the back. "Well done, my friend. Have you decided on the wedding plans or am I being premature?"

"Well, with your permission, we'd like to be wed at Krikor after it's rebuilt."

"We'd be most honored." Avery shook the dwarf's hand in agreement.

"I can hardly wait," Angel declared and hugged him.

"Good," Barak interrupted. "Since we're all standing around, we might as well discuss what to do next."

"I'll hunt up the major," Devlak added. Before he left, however, Dwarflord Boden asked him to bring back Ervin Blockman, the Boman's quarry master.

"Let's all gather at the main campfire for the meeting. At least, that's where the coffee will be."

"Angel and I will make the coffee," Kalika hurriedly put in.

Barak led the way. Angel observed the hustle and bustle occurring around them as they strode to the fire. The dwarves, men, and elves surrounded campfires in peaceful comradeship. It was a very good sight, to be sure.

At the main campfire, Barak sent for more mugs and food. When everyone ate their fill and held full mugs of fresh coffee, the meeting got underway. It lasted about three hours. Afterward, Dwarflord Boden sent some of his men back into Boman for building supplies.

They were leaving for Krikor and the city's rebuild in the morning.

CHAPTER 12

New Krikor

SEPTEMBER 2 TURNED INTO A beautiful day. The entourage of dwarves, men, and elves arrived at the ruins of Krikor shortly before lunchtime. A fierce storm had caught them a few days earlier. All were grateful for the warm noonday sun. The first order of business was to erect a tent city on the outskirts for the workers. Three-quarters of the Bomani dwarves came to help. The tent city went up in a matter of hours. The workers set up the kitchens and storage tents nearest the work area. The sleeping tents were raised a few hundred yards away from where the noise of the workers wouldn't disturb the day sleepers. To honor the hard work the elves had put in on helping free Boman, the Bomani dwarves decided work would be continuous.

It amazed Angel how "gung-ho" the dwarves were. They decided tomorrow they would begin the castle clean-up. But some of the younger dwarves had already started that chore having finished erecting their tents. They seemed tireless to her.

I guess after being cooped up for nearly nine months anyone would be 'antsy,' she thought.

Niedra strode up and rubbed against Angel's leg. *Man not as afraid of us now. Some let us help. That is very good.*

"Yes, it is, my feline friend," Angel said aloud. She petted the huge head. *We've made a difference on how man sees your kind.* She snuggled against the cat, her head touching Niedra's. *We cleared up a lot of misunderstandings between both species, haven't we?*

The huge cat purred. *My sibs know man's words now but man doesn't know ours. Man can't talk to all of us. Only you.*

Angel watched the work being done on the castle and straightened. *I just had an idea, Niedra. See how the dwarves use hand signals sometimes? We need something like that, a similar language for man and cat.*

Yes. That is good idea, my man friend. Niedra mewed one last time, rose and padded off to join the other cats.

Angel chuckled. To the cat, they were all 'man' no matter the sex or race. But the cat seemed to understand the word 'similar.' *What a place this could become if only the world stayed this way now,* she thought. *That is one lesson the badgercats could teach us. If a badgercat could learn from us, couldn't we learn from them?*

The dwarves had wasted no time in planning out four shifts. Each shift worked twelve hours and overlapped each other by six hours. So, at any one time two shifts were working. Torches went up everywhere and illuminated the area, especially the castle ruins. More and more dwarves took up the work of moving rubble. Soon, in the tent city, workers were either returning from the castle or getting ready for their own shifts. Even the kitchens, working nonstop, arranged their own shifts. The Bomani women tended the men along with doing the laundry and keeping the washing areas behind the kitchens cleaned and stocked with supplies.

It was getting dark when Avery sauntered up. "You look like you're thinking hard about something. You aren't worried, are you?"

Angel smiled and shook her head. "No. I'm just amazed at the bustle going on."

Avery took her hand. "Ready to retire? Mom and dad are tucked into their tent. We have one next door to theirs."

She sighed. "Yes, it's been a long day." She quietly watched her animal protector as it ambled up with the Lunn brothers' two pets. *Niedra, we're going to sleep. Help Merr and Derr keep the other cats in harmony with man. Make sure there's no fights tonight.*

Harmony? Yes, nice to each other. No fights. I understand. Three of us, four wild cats.

Angel laughed quietly. "Goodnight, Niedra," she said aloud. Harmony, a new word for the cat. And, she picked up the meaning fast. Yes, those cats were definitely getting smarter.

Niedra mewed and left.

She and Avery entered their tent and retired for the night. She felt safer this night than she had in a long time and thought about the past few weeks. Her children were now safe in Damek or on their way here. Her husband lay next to her and had fallen asleep almost immediately. And the threat of Ahriman was finally over. It was a good time. She turned onto her side and watched Avery for a while before closing her own eyes. Outside, she heard the bustle of working dwarves and hoped it would lull her to sleep.

But that was not to be. Angel's head overflowed with so many ideas. After an hour of tossing, she carefully got out of bed to avoid waking Avery and stepped out of the tent to a clear, crisp night. She spotted both of Cornellius's falcons roosting atop his tent.

Niedra and two other cats lay at the entrance. All three looked up at her and purred. She noticed Niedra had chosen the two wildest of her four siblings, Jakko and the unattached cat, as her "partners." Her two offspring took care of the two tamer wild cats. She caught sight of them lounging out in the darkness a little behind her own tent.

She patted Niedra's head in assurance and glanced skyward.

How's everything? She asked the cat.

Fine. Niedra looked up at her. *Angel?*

Startled, Angel looked at Niedra. *Definitely getting too smart,* she reflected to herself. To Niedra, she thought, *You've never used my name before. What do you want?*

Man use name. Do you not like?

Oh, I like very much, my dear friend. You honor me.

Honor?

Makes me feel special.

I understand. Zolia wants Ariel. The third cat mewed. *She is Zolia,* Niedra added.

Does she hear Ariel's mind?

Yes, Zolia thought to her. *I hear her before she left. I think about her a lot now.*

Angel smiled. *I guess I'll talk to Ariel when she arrives. But you will have to be there, also.*

Call me and I will be there. Thank you, Angel. Zolia lowered her head in tribute.

Angel sat down and leaned against Niedra. *Do you think with Merr and Derr's help and their men, we can come up with a cat language all can learn?*

Yes. Jamala, too, when she returns. All cats talk about it after you said it to me.

Another new word, my friend? You listen to man well.

Yes. Know man that way. I teach other cats to listen, too. Jakko and Zolia mewed their agreement.

Tomorrow we will start a new language beneficial to both species. She wondered how Niedra would react to the new words as she thought to the cat, *even your siblings.*

Yes. Thank you Angel. From us all. The cats purred.

"Well," Angel whispered. "Goodnight, you three." She reentered the tent with their soft mews following her. She felt so safe with the three badgercats protecting them that night. She snuggled up to her husband and fell fast asleep.

———— ∞∞∞∞∞∞∞∞∞∞ ————

The next morning found more supplies and men arriving from Damek. Along with the supplies, Nicholas returned the twins and Ariel safely to Angel. He had a surprise for his uncle, too. Queen Elena had accompanied them. Excited to see his new bride, Cornellius took her to his tent for a heartfelt reunion. Friends and family gathered around the main kitchen fire. The dwarf women served steaming fresh mugs of coffee to the adults. The twins received big glasses of fruit juice. Jamala padded up to Niedra and touched noses. The cats acknowledged each other before settling with their prospective human mates.

Angel quietly chuckled at Nicholas as he watched the interchange between the cats. "With the Lunn brothers' help, we're devising a kind of language between man and beast so all can communicate," she told him. "The cats teach me their mews and I pass it along. Anyone interested in learning can join in. Maybe we can start a new trade."

"Fascinating." Nicholas shook his head in wonderment. "Okay. I've got a question. Why are you using rock in the castle walls? I thought you were going to rebuild Krikor as before."

"This will make Krikor less vulnerable. Besides, Dwarflord Boden gave us the idea of using the rocks and boulders we dug away from the Boman cavern entrance. Since beginning the clean-up, he's had some of his men traveling back and forth hauling the debris here. It makes

Krikor a type of shrine to the elves and dwarves, to remind all of the hardship both endured."

"At this speed, we plan to be finished roughly by the first of December," Serylda announced, joining them.

"I don't doubt that." Nicholas looked over at the dwarf. "You, too, Serylda?" he commented.

When he pointed at the cat beside her then at her, Serylda smiled. "Meet Gran."

"Hello, Gran." After the cat mewed at him, Nicholas grunted and glanced around. "How are you feeding this crowd?"

Cornellius and Elena strode up as Cornellius answered, "The Falconlanders are using their birds in harvesting fresh meat for stews. Speaking of falcons, I have a job I'd like your help with, Nicholas."

Before Cornellius announced the job for Nicholas, a young dwarf girl arrived with two more mugs and fresh coffee. She refilled the mugs. Behind her another maiden arrived with a tray laden with fresh fruit and cheeses. She set the tray down and both maidens left. The group spent a few moments eating and drinking the light breakfast. When the tray was empty, another pot of coffee was brought over and mugs were once again refilled. The tray disappeared with the empty coffeepot.

"Uncle, before you tell me of this job, I want to talk to you." Nicholas relaxed against a tree.

"What about?"

"I want to say thank you for giving me the responsibility of leading men to Damek. They had become my army during the trek to Damek even though they consisted of dwarves. I realize I've done a lot of growing up on the journey. I believe you had put me in charge to build my self-confidence and to learn responsibility. When Angel had instructed me on the use of the Geiger counter and then you had put me in charge of the army, I had felt overwhelmed. No longer do I feel that way. I just wanted you to know this."

Cornellius slapped his nephew on the back and laughed heartily. "You've grown into a fine young man. I'm proud of you."

"Now, uncle, tell me of the job you wanted my help with."

"As you know, you're old enough to begin training falcons in the hope of owning one yourself, if you so desire. Since I have two very young ones who need training, I'd like your help. I'm not sure if I want to keep one or both. First, I need to train them before I decide. Since they've been through a lot, they may need to stay together. Hence your help. Besides, it will bode well for you."

Nicholas grinned. "I'm game. Who knows? You may set a new trend, keeping two instead of the traditional one."

Cornellius rose. "Let's get started now. My shift doesn't begin for another three hours."

Angel rose, too. "Elena, would you like to join Alison and myself? We go to help in the laundry."

"My pleasure!" Elena jumped up and followed. "I had hoped there would be something for me to do here."

Angel felt the relief in Elena to be able to do something useful. Everyone rose and each went their separate ways.

The next day the supplies from Jasper arrived led by Dwarflady Morna and General Mandek. Barak went off with his spouse for some private time. The general joined his forces with the workers from Boman and Falconland. They were as eager as the others to get their hands dirty, too.

—————w∞α℧ℴ⟆ℴ⟆ℴ⟆∞ℴm—————

A cheer rose from the crowd as former queen Kalika Soren placed the last stone in the castle wall. It was finished and it was 10:00 a.m. on the last day of November in New Krikor. Celebrations were planned for the rest of the day. The last shift officially ended at noon.

Over the next seven days, the people returned to their new homes. Before everyone left, however, a major celebration took place. Three couples married, but not at the same time. Each was special. First to wed was Devlak to Raven Greyrock. Devlak agreed to call Boman home. In reciprocation, Dwarflord Boden made Devlak his heir and consequently, the next heir to the Boman throne. This deed brought the two dwarf settlements back together as one people. All Bomani dwarves celebrated the good news.

Cornellius gave Nicholas his choice of one of the two falcons for a wedding gift when he and Ariel married next. Nicholas named his new companion Centa after Kalika's people. Kalika felt deep humbleness from the deed and thanked him for the honor. The couple chose to stay at New Krikor and help the ones still needing homes built. Ariel still took care of the twins. As a wedding gift, the cats lined up in front of the couple. Angel introduced Ariel to Zolia. Both human and cat joined immediately. Zolia's rough nature softened in exposure with Ariel's quiet one. In reciprocation, the cat gave Ariel confidence she never had before.

Lastly, Alison married the Falconlander Geoff Dakota who she fell in love with during the rebuild. Serylda forgave her for the part she played during the evil times. She accepted the privilege of being Alison's maid-of-honor. Both became close friends during the castle rebuild. Alison and Geoff decided Damek was the place for them. Cornellius asked what they wanted for a wedding gift. Geoff wanted to train a falcon for his own. Alison liked the idea so much that she asked for the same thing. She became the first woman to train her own, setting a new trend in Falconland, and in the land in general. Not only did she train a falcon but she also had the faithful cat Jakko for a companion.

Serylda learned of Dag Ironstone's love for her. She told him she might marry him when they returned to Jasper. Galinia, her mother, would like that they would perhaps marry in Jasper. But she had a few things to work out in her own head before she could marry him. Angel sensed in Serylda's heart that she still mourned Javas Ozuna. Weeks earlier, Serylda had confided in Angel about the man she thought she loved. It had been Dag all along.

Serylda just wanted him to think of one thing before they married, if they did. She wanted to raise their own company of soldiers and march to Amar. She wanted that town respectable for a number of reasons. One was making that town theirs. It was about time Amar joined the rest of the country. Secondly, she wanted to tame the town for the twins' sake. He agreed wholeheartedly.

A month passed quickly. Angel noticed the old queen, Kalika, was looking sick. She found her under an apple tree on January 2.

"Are you okay, Mother?" she asked. She began calling Kalika mother shortly after New Krikor was built.

Kalika smiled and nodded. "I'm feeling my years, child. My ancestors are calling me." She softly chuckled. "I have no ancestors here. They lived on another world. Help me up and let's take a walk."

They walked slowly for twenty minutes away from everyone. After finding a fallen log, they sat down.

"I don't want to alarm you, but I think I have only two or three weeks left," Kalika admitted.

Angel gasped. "So soon?"

"We Centauri know almost to the day when our life is coming to an end. We age and die within a week's time, earth time." She took a deep breath and let it out slowly. "There is something I didn't inform you of. The day I helped you defeat Stormy, I had sent a piece of myself to bind the Zaxcellian into the wolf. In doing so, I shortened my lifespan by several hundred years. What surprised me is having that ability in the first place. But I felt my life essence diminish as I did the deed."

"Now, you are dying?" Angel asked astonished.

She patted Angel's hand. "It was worth the sacrifice to know you are safe from my enemy. I've already informed Iomar about the time I have left."

"What if you die before we get you to the Great Crack? Won't you disappear like Ahriman did?"

"I will lock a piece of myself inside your crystal which will keep my body near you. When you enter the Great Crack, it will return to my body."

Angel nodded. They sat in comfortable silence for a few minutes after Kalika performed the deed.

"I want to tell you a few things before it's too late." Kalika took a breath. "I'm glad the mariners from Europe have found this continent. It bodes well that your world will once more become united. Nicholas proved to be an excellent diplomat."

Angel laughed. "It was a surprise for us all. He's a pretty smooth talker, the perfect ambassador. Ariel is glad he's back."

Kalika took hold of Angel's right hand. "The human race was stronger than we Centauri imagined. I wish I wasn't the last of my race here. At least the threat we brought your world is over." She let Angel's hand go. "Well, I hope it is."

Angel frowned. That apprehensive feeling was coming back. "What do you mean by that?"

"I wasn't going to say anything but you need to know this. We Centauri lied about Ahriman. I knew Ahriman was being controlled by an evil entity, the Zaxcellian I mentioned at an earlier time. I was sure of this when you defeated Ahriman and the entity entered your sister. He had us fooled until then. I let him think he still fooled us when your sister was in his grasp."

"Why did you keep this secret?" Angel asked quietly.

"For one thing, your world is hard to find. We weren't worried about them finding this world. But, as you know now, one stole aboard our ship. If he never had contact with his world, your world is safe. I can't trust he didn't. Someone on this world needs to know the possible threat." She shook her head slowly. "I'm terribly sorry for keeping this a secret. Forgive me."

Angel smiled. "There's nothing to forgive. I've learned how kind your species is. All you ever did was try to help this world. I'll never forget that, nor allow anyone else to either."

Kalika smiled back. "You are kind to an old woman."

"Can you answer me one question?" At Kalika's nod, Angel continued, "I've wondered if the badgercats have always had the ability to hear thoughts of other beings. Perhaps on Centaurus, they did so universally?"

"In my deepest memories, I have a feeling they did. But, it being so long ago, I can't reassure you that that's the norm for the animal."

Angel sighed. "Ever since the twins returned from Amar, Janna said she hears Jamala. And it seemed strange when I learned the wild cats wanted to become partners to certain people. I can hear all of them, though they can only hear myself and one other."

"It is a nice surprise. How did Barak react when Seth told him he wanted to partner him? I was never told."

"He didn't know if he wanted the partnership or not. It amazed him when he heard Seth in his mind."

"I'm glad one wanted to partner him. Especially with the experience he had endured."

"I'm still amazed that I alone can hear them all."

"Perhaps it's the side effects of your crystal."

Angel nodded in agreement. "That's the only explanation I can come up with. I tried to mind talk with Cornellius's falcons and couldn't. It seems my gift only works with people and the badgercats." She looked at the ground a moment. "Remember when you looked into Alison's mind to see how she coped with being in the Zaxcellian's control for so long?

Can you do something similar to see why I can hear the cats? To see if it is indeed the crystal?"

"That was different. I can only tell if the Zaxcellian left any residual piece of itself. I cannot tell if the crystal is the reason behind your abilities. But your gift to hear the cats may truly be the result of your crystal."

She grinned. "It was a thought." She took hold of the old woman's hand, rose, and helped the old Centauri up. "Come. We should get back. Your hands are cold."

"I have one wish before I leave this world. I'd like the Kaliborn elves to join us at the Great Crack when the time comes to return me there. They deserve the closure as much as you do."

"I will inform Avery when we get back inside," Angel promised as they slowly made their way back to the castle.

When Angel relayed the Centauri's wishes to Avery, he decided to send two men each to Jasper, Kaliborn, Boman and Damek. He charged the men to ask for the leaders of Boman and Damek to join them at New Krikor as soon as possible, while the Jasper and Kaliborn leaders were to meet them at the Great Crack. They were to tell them Kalika was dying.

⸻ ‧₊˚⊹ ⸻

On January 25, an assembly was called in the Great Hall. Dwarflord Boden and his wife Gem, along with their daughter Raven and her husband Devlak, were the only ones from Boman to attend. Of the Falconlanders, Cornellius and Elena arrived before the dwarves. Alison and Geoff had accompanied them. Since Nicholas lived in New Krikor with Ariel, they had helped set up for the assembly.

On the throne sat the ancient couple once more. Angel and Avery stood on either side. With Angel's help, Kalika rose and walked to the edge of the dais and addressed the Elfin Nation one last time.

"I once told Queen Angel the human race is stronger than we Centauri thought. I wish I wasn't the last of my species. You could teach my people a thing or two. At least I saw the end of the evil we brought to your world. That threat is over. And so is my time upon this world. I give my blessing upon all species of this planet. May it ever be safe from invaders."

As she made her way back to the throne, she said to Angel, "I'm glad I told you of the threat of the Zaxcellians, our most hated enemy. One had possessed first Ahriman, then your sister, Alison. I'm sorry for the trouble he caused you and your sister. I'm glad it didn't last and that you both are steadfast in your love for each other. I hope with my last breath the Zaxcellians never find this world."

Angel helped her sit back down. The old couple clasped hands. The ancient Centauri smiled at the assembly, then taking one last breath bowed her head and quietly died, Iomar still holding her hand. No one mourned her passing. She didn't want that. Angel reminded everyone of the goodness the Centauri embodied and how the people of the earth should be grateful.

On January 30, five days after her passing, they carefully wrapped Kalika's body and a trek to the Great Crack was once again underway. The entire Elfin Nation accompanied the body. The Bomani dwarves at New Krikor joined them.

On the way, the old king fell ill. Avery promised his father he would be buried with Kalika if he didn't make it to the Great Crack. Sadly, it turned out to be the case. He died on March 24, eight days from their destination.

They were met by the entire nation of Kaliborn and a select few from Jasper when they arrived at the Great Crack. The Kaliborn had turned up one day earlier whereas the Jasper dwarves had set up camp a few days before that.

A small memorial took place before a select few descended the cliff. Twenty four persons accompanied the bodies on the way down. The elves consisted of Avery, Angel, the twins, the Lunn brothers, and Ariel of New Krikor. From Kaliborn, Queen Lorina and King Selik with their son Varik and his wife Timil were next. Timil had joined in the trek to the Great Crack though her baby was due any time. She planned to name their child Kalika after the Centauri who was responsible for their colony.

Ariel's husband Nicholas, along with King and Queen Fraomar, and Geoff and Alison Dakota made up the Falconlanders. The dwarves who attended came from both cavern systems. From Jasper, Barak and Morna paid their respects with Serylda and her new husband, Dag. Barak's brother, Devlak, and his wife Raven, now living at Boman, had accompanied Dwarflord Boden and Dwarflady Gem.

Eight badgercats, with Niedra in charge, sat atop the cliff as the attendants made their way down to the Ancient Ones' cave. Angel led the way into the cave. On the trek through the caverns, Angel felt the piece of Kalika that had resided inside her crystal return to the Centauri. Once inside the living quarters, everyone walked quietly by the Centauri lined up along the wall. The pallbearers placed Kalika next to Zema. Her last husband was laid to rest at her feet.

"Well, one era ends and another begins," Angel said. "We shall never forget where we came from or what has happened."

"To insure that," added Dwarflord Boden, "the dwarf nation will carve a memorial in honor of the Centauri and it will reside in New Krikor."

Angel thanked the Dwarflord for the promised gift. The entourage formed a line and once more solemnly walked past the line of Centauri ending at Kalika. Without stopping, they made their way out of the cavern and up the canyon. Angel brought up the rear. The first thing she noticed was time hadn't changed on this occasion and wondered why.

When they all reached the canyon rim, in unison, the cats gave a loud screech. Moments later, a noise not unlike thunder, rolled through the canyon.

"The caverns have collapsed," Angel said to all. "Kalika told me when all her kind here on earth were finally entombed below, this would happen."

Avery faced the crowd. The cats encircled him and Angel who stood nearby.

"It is the beginning of a new era," he said. "Let us hope we don't make a mess of things. Let's go home."

As everyone said their goodbyes before leaving for their respective homes, Angel thought about all that had happened to her since becoming a member of this time. She was happy and had her sister back. And, she had good friends, some who were badgercats. The Kaliborn elves were no longer a secret. Angel promised Queen Lorina they would never again be forgotten. They were now a part of the societies of the world.

She smiled and took her husband's hand. Yes, life was definitely good.

ABOUT THE AUTHOR

D EBBIE NORDMAN IS A STAY-AT-HOME wife. She enjoyed inventing stories for her siblings as a child. The Alastrine Legend series came about from a dream of an unusual creature that became the badgercat in her book. She lives in Odessa, Texas with her husband of over 30 happy years.